Gamers' Rebellion

George Ivanoff is an author and stay-at-home dad residing in Melbourne, Australia. He has written over 60 books for children and teenagers. His teen science fiction novel, *Gamers' Quest*, won a 2010 Chronos Award for speculative fiction. He has books on both the Victorian Premier's and the NSW Premier's Reading Challenge booklists. George eats too much chocolate and drinks too much coffee. He has one wife and two children.

Visit George's website at:
georgeivanoff.com.au
and the Gamers website:
www.gamersquestbook.com

For my godson
Nicholas Ernst
with much love

THE GAMERS' TRILOGY

Gamers' Quest
Gamers' Challenge
Gamers' Rebellion
'Gamers' Inferno' is also in *Trust Me Too*,
edited by Paul Collins

GAMERS' REBELLION

George Ivanoff

FORD ST

First published by Ford Street Publishing, an imprint of
Hybrid Publishers, PO Box 52, Ormond VIC 3204
Melbourne Victoria Australia
www.hybridpublishers.com.au

© George Ivanoff 2013
2 4 6 8 10 9 7 5 3 1

This publication is copyright. Apart from any use
as permitted under the Copyright Act 1968, no part
may be reproduced by any process without prior written
permission from the publisher. Requests and enquiries
concerning reproduction should be addressed to
Ford Street Publishing Pty Ltd
2 Ford Street, Clifton Hill VIC 3068.
Ford Street website: www.fordstreetpublishing.com

First published 2013

National Library of Australia Cataloguing-in-Publication entry
Author: Ivanoff, George, 1968–
Title: Gamers' rebellion / George Ivanoff.
ISBN: 9781921665974 (pbk.)
Target Audience: For secondary school age.
Dewey Number: A823.3

Cover art: Les Petersen
Cover design: © Gittus Graphics
In-house editor: Beau Hillier

Printed in China by Tingleman Pty Ltd

Contents

Prologue	1
1: Tark	2
2: Zyra	6
3: Escape	9
4: Captured	11
5: Wake Up	16
6: Administrators	19
7: Josie and the Rebels	26
8: Designer Prime	29
9: People Who Don't Matter	45
10: Mel	49
11: Food	61
12: The Game	66
13: Desert Sands	73
14: Into the Game	78
15: Machines	81
16: Kiss	89
17: Children	94
18: Back In	101
19: Designer Alpha	104

20: Hidden	113
21: Reunion	117
22: Designing	129
23: Return of the Ultimate Gamer	134
24: Reprogram	150
25: On the Inside	152
26: We Have a Problem	159
27: Back in the Lab	161
28: Beta and Tark	165
29: Portal Battle	173
30: Hope	179
31: The Plan	184
32: The Outers	192
33: Breakdown Begins	196
34: Exit	199
35: Josie and Tark	203
36: Downloading	206
37: Calming Down	211
38: The Rebellion	213
39: Alex	223
40: Designer Beta	226
41: Containment Breakout	232
42: Preserving Unreality	237
Epilogue	244
Acknowledgments	245

Prologue

The game was over! Or so they thought.

With hands tightly clasped, Tark and Zyra watched as all they had ever known melted away.

And then they were moving through greyness. It was like swimming through treacle. Up ahead, two intense points of white light called to them.

The greyness swirled around them, tugging and pulling.

Their fingers slipped and their hands parted. They were whisked away from each other and towards the light – towards the unknown.

1: Tark

Tark felt like he was drowning.

He tried coughing and gasping for air, but the warm, viscous liquid surrounded him. He opened his mouth and more of it flowed in and filled his lungs.

Tark's eyes snapped open. Everything was glowing, soft-focus, green nothingness. Panic set in. He thrashed his arms and legs about, connecting with what felt like skin.

Forcing himself to calm down, he reached out with more care. Whatever it was, it was all around him, like a cocoon encasing him in an environment of fluid – like a baby in a womb. He pushed his hands forward and felt the skin stretch and distend. No, not skin. More like something synthetic ... plastic or rubber.

With a sudden burst of hope, Tark pushed his fingers into it, feeling it stretch further. He put more pressure against it and curled his fingers into fists, grasping the rubbery substance and pulling. He felt it beginning to give. Doubling his efforts, he pushed, pulled and clawed at it until it gave way, rending apart.

The fluid suddenly drained away and Tark coughed, expelling a lungful of thick green liquid. Then he gasped, drawing in huge, rasping lungfuls of air. His mind was spinning. He blinked rapidly, then wiped the last of the ooze from his eyes.

He was lying on a hard floor in a pool of liquid, the tattered remains of the membrane clinging to his skin like a burst balloon. Tubes and wires rested beside him, snaking across the floor and connecting into the wall. Tark lifted his head. He was in the middle of a stark white room, with one mirrored wall. Harsh, bright light flooded down from the ceiling.

Tark coughed uncontrollably, the last of the fluid coming up from his lungs. And then he retched, spewing up a stomachful of the horrid stuff into the green ooze that he was still lying in.

Desperate to get out of the puddle, vomit still dribbling from the corners of his mouth, he tried to get up. His legs wobbled like jelly and slipped in the pooling liquid. He fell face first into the green slime. Thrashing about, he managed to steady himself. He vomited again, this time a thin stream of green slime mixed with yellowish bile.

He groaned. And then a torrent of warm water rained down on him. It was the first pleasant sensation since he emerged from the cocoon. But it didn't last.

As the rain ceased, he watched the last of the green wash away down a grating in the floor. The surface then sealed up over it.

Concentrating hard, Tark forced a leg under himself. Then the other. Closing his eyes, he pushed himself up onto his hands and knees. Pins and needles prickled through his arms and legs, but at least he could feel them. He felt his strength slowly returning.

A gust of warm air blew through the room, drying everything.

Tark pulled back into a crouching position, and from there he unsteadily got to his feet. He took a deep breath to calm himself, suppressing a cough, then took a wobbly step forward. Then another. He felt himself rapidly steadying as the pins and needles faded.

He took another deep breath and opened his eyes.

Tark almost fell back down in surprise.

The reflection that greeted him was not his own. The image in the mirror was tall and lithe. And naked. Tark's eyes moved from the brown, wavy hair and familiar face, down the defined musculature.

He lifted an arm, the muscles tensing and bulging. He extended his hand and waved it. The image followed suit. It was him, even though it did not look like him. He looked almost like John Hayes, the avatar he used when in the Suburbia environment with Zyra. Almost, but not quite. He looked like an idealised version of John Hayes – flawless skin and perfect physique. He was the 16-year-old that every teenage boy longed to be.

Tark wondered if he had somehow wound up in the Suburbia environment. He glanced around the sterile room. He didn't remember anything like this in Suburbia. And he was supposed to be out of the game, completely. Wasn't he?

And where was Zyra? Why wasn't she with him? They had left the game together. Had he somehow been pulled back in? Was he trapped in some other environment, forced into an avatar and destined to play yet another of the Designers' seemingly endless games within games?

Tark looked back at his reflection as these thoughts tumbled through his mind. He opened his mouth, ready to test out his voice.

A high-pitched wailing split the silence. And everything went dark.

2: Zyra

Zyra stood in front of the mirrored wall as the gust of warm air subsided, staring at the reflection that was not her. She was supposed to have a red Mohawk and piercings and green eyes and …

She knew that the familiar blonde-haired image must be her, because it raised its arm as she raised hers and inclined its head as she did hers. She stared into the eyes of a girl that was a perfect version of Tina Burrows, her Suburbia avatar.

Behind her image, she saw a portion of the white wall open up. A person stepped into the room. She turned around, ready, as always, for a fight.

A strange boy stood by the far wall, which was solid once more. He was shorter than her and dressed in grey clothing that clung to him like a second skin. He had a white garment draped over one arm. He was bald, which made it difficult for Zyra to guess at his age. Fifteen?

'This is for you,' he said, stepping forward and

holding out the clothing, eyes wide.

Zyra was suddenly conscious that she was naked. She dashed forward, snatched the garment from his hand and held it up against herself. Seeing her discomfort, the boy turned his back to her.

Zyra quickly shook out the garment and examined it. It was a jumpsuit, similar to the one the boy was wearing, but it looked much too small to fit her. She stepped into it anyway, pulling it up over herself, the odd plastic-like fabric stretching to accommodate her body. It covered her feet and extended into gloves that enveloped her hands. She pulled the two sides of fabric towards each other, wondering how to do up the suit since there was no zip or buttons. The fabric simply merged into itself, closing up the gap and leaving no visible join.

Zyra flexed her arms and wiggled her fingers, marvelling at the surprising comfort of the outfit. It was like being naked and clothed at the same time.

'How do I go to the toilet in this thing?' she wondered out loud.

'It is a smart fabric,' explained the boy in quiet, measured tones. 'It has automatically coded itself to your genetic makeup. It will come apart for you, if you pull at it.'

The boy turned around. Zyra noticed that he was more than just bald – he was completely hairless. No eyebrows, no eyelashes, not even the shadow of shaved hair. His eyes were the palest blue she had ever seen, and they were focused intently on her.

'Where am I?' asked Zyra.

'Specifically,' said the boy, 'you are in the Design Institute. On a more general level, you are in what you would term *the real world*.'

'What?'

'You are no longer in the Game.'

Zyra frowned, taking in the enormity of the revelation. Fixing her eyes on the boy, she felt a shiver go up her spine.

'Are you … are you a Designer?'

'No,' the boy answered. 'I am not.'

Before Zyra had time to react, an alarm started blaring, the high-pitched wailing hurting her ears. And everything went dark.

3: Escape

Completely disorientated, Tark stumbled about in the dark, the alarm blaring around him. He crashed into one of the walls and cried out, clutching his bruised elbow.

A portion of the wall slid back and dimly silhouetted figures rushed into the room. Hands grabbed at him and something was thrown over his head. He tried to struggle, lashing out at his assailants. His arms were seized roughly and pinned behind him. Tark leaned his weight back, using his captor for support, and kicked out with both his legs.

Someone swore, then another assailant grasped Tark's legs and he was manhandled towards the door. He continued to struggle, thrashing about.

'Lets go of me,' he shouted. If he had not been so preoccupied, he would have marvelled at the sound of the voice that was nothing like his own.

'Shut him up,' someone hissed.

Tark felt something cold and metallic pressed to

his side. There was an audible crackle and he felt a jolt of electricity course through his body.

He passed out.

***

Tark ached – from the tip of his nose to the ends of his toes. Slowly, his awareness widened and he felt movement. He was being carried, jostled about roughly as his kidnappers ran with him. Nausea washed over him. He tried breathing deeply to suppress it.

He opened his eyes but saw nothing. Something still covered his head.

And then he heard the voices. Urgent, hissing voices over the top of one another, making it difficult to understand anything.

'… got to get out …'

'… he's heavy …'

'… which way?'

'… what about the other one?'

'… too late …'

'… damn …'

He felt the hands holding his left leg slip, and the heel of his foot scraped along the ground. Tark yelped.

'He's awake!' The voice was panicky.

'Zap him!' ordered a more authoritative voice.

Again, Tark felt the metal pressing up against him before the shock of electricity sent him into oblivion.

4: Captured

Zyra crouched in the darkness, every muscle tense, ready to spring at the first sign of trouble.

'Do not panic!' said the boy, his voice calm and steady as the alarm blared. 'You are quite safe.'

'I don't panic,' said Zyra, matter-of-factly, wishing she had her knives and feeling exposed in her clinging jumpsuit.

A square of dim light appeared at the far wall as the door slid open, revealing three silhouettes. Before any of them could make a move, the boy was blocking their entrance.

'No!' he said, his voice still calm. 'Zyra must stay here.'

'Guards,' warned one of the silhouettes. Then all three sped off.

Zyra saw other shadows running past the doorway before it closed. Then the lights came back on.

Zyra stood up. 'What just happened?' she demanded.

'It appears we have had an attempted abduction,' said the boy.

'Why would someone want to kidnap me?' asked Zyra.

'Good question,' said the boy.

'And where's Tark?'

'Another good question.'

Zyra's expression hardened. 'So how about some good answers, kid?' She took a threatening step towards the boy.

'I would rather not be referred to as *kid*.' The boy inclined his head slightly. 'I am not a kid – not in the conventional sense. I am a clone. And my name is Robbie.'

'Yeah, well that's great, *Robbie*. But I want some answers.' Zyra took another step. 'And I want them now.'

'Please remain calm,' said Robbie. 'My purpose in being here is to introduce you to the real world and give you all the necessary information. So please, let us sit down and discuss things.'

Two white spherical chairs emerged from behind opening wall panels, and slid towards them. The panels closed up as if they had never been there. Robbie sat down immediately, nodding towards the second chair. Zyra sat down warily.

'Okay, I'm sitting. I'm calm. Now, get on with it.'

'You are in a scientific facility and research centre called –'

'Where's Tark?' Zyra cut him off. 'I want to see him.'

Robbie paused and cocked his head to one side as if considering Zyra's question.

'Tark is in a clone birthing room like this one. You cannot see him yet. You –'

'Why can't I see him?' demanded Zyra, cutting him off again. 'If he's here then I want to see him, now!'

'I am sorry,' said Robbie. 'There are procedures to be followed. You need to be debriefed before anything else can happen.'

'Right.' Zyra crossed her arms. 'Get on with it then.'

'As I have already said, you are out of the Game – you are in the real world.'

Zyra held her hands up in front of her face. They were encased in the weird, skin-like fabric. She turned them over and then back again, flexing the fingers and letting the words sink in – *the real world*.

'No doubt you are wondering, *how?*' said Robbie. 'You have been downloaded into a cloned body.'

Zyra lowered her hands and stared at Robbie. 'Like you?'

'Not quite.' Although Robbie's expression remained constant, Zyra thought she caught a hint of sadness in his eyes. 'Your cloned body was specifically prepared for a downloaded consciousness. That is, it was grown from the cells of a real person, but was conditioned for physical perfection. It was also grown with no cognitive functions. Your body has a brain, but it was a *tabula rasa* – a clean slate onto which anything could have been written.'

'And I was written onto it,' said Zyra. 'So, how is that different from you?'

'I was entirely cloned. My cognitive functions are a copy of my original. As is my physical … non-perfection. But I have been conditioned as a robot.'

'How can you be a robot if you're a clone?' Zyra asked. 'Aren't robots mechanical?'

'The word robot simply refers to an entity created to perform specific tasks. That is what I am, officially.' Robbie lowered his eyes. 'My emotional development has been inhibited. Certain physical characteristics have been genetically imposed as a designation of my status.' Robbie's hand briefly went to stroke the skin where an eyebrow should have been.

'I have intelligence. However, my thought processes and my decisions mirror those of my originator, Designer Prime.'

'The Designers are here!' Zyra's eyes were wide with excitement.

'Yes.'

'Take me to them.' Zyra jumped to her feet expectantly. 'I want to see them.'

'I am afraid things do not work like that,' said Robbie. 'There is a hierarchy to be observed.'

'What's that supposed to mean?'

'It means you have to wait until someone is ready to see you.'

'And how long will that take?'

'Given that it is currently 2 am, it may be a while.'

As if in response a harsh electronic voice boomed all around them: 'Downloaded entity known as Zyra to be brought to administration room 12.'

'Or perhaps not.' Robbie stood up. 'Please follow me.' He walked towards the doorway that had again opened up in the far wall.

Zyra followed, wondering what the Designers would look like.

5: Wake Up

Tark woke up and felt pain – all over. He took a deep breath and even that hurt. And his arm felt as if someone was stabbing it repeatedly.

He heard voices and the bustle of movement.

'Found the vein.'

'Measurements?'

'Check.'

'Cell sample?'

'Check.'

'Hair?'

'Yep.'

'Blood?'

Tark could hardly move. He felt himself being prodded and poked, so he forced himself to open his eyes.

With his head lolling to one side, the first thing he saw was a kid with red hair. The boy held up a syringe full of blood.

'Finally got it.' The kid smiled and then noticed

Tark's eyes were open. He jumped back, fumbling with the syringe, almost dropping it, and catching it again at the last moment.

'He's awake,' the boy yelped.

'Okay, back off,' said a voice that was out of his line of sight.

The kid moved away.

With a great deal of effort, Tark managed to move his head. He caught sight of two other kids, one boy and one girl. Tark noticed that they were all wearing lab coats. What were they doing to him? Experimenting on him? Stealing his blood? Getting ready to dissect him?

He tried to call out, but all he managed was an incoherent grunt.

'He still can't move properly,' said the older boy, approaching Tark. 'We've probably got a few minutes to finish up. Get the samples into the cooler.'

The younger boy looked at the syringe of blood – Tark's blood – and then moved to the other end of the room. The girl, who was holding a Petri dish and a glass slide, also moved off. The older boy continued to stare at Tark.

'Tara, set up the last scan,' the boy ordered.

'And Len, go get the boss.'

The younger boy raced off.

The older boy moved around to the head of the table. He put his hands on either side of Tark's head and straightened it so that Tark was looking up towards the ceiling – except that his view of the ceiling was blocked by some sort of machine. A machine that was descending towards him.

Tark tried to move, to jump up from the table and run off, but all he managed to do was twitch his arms and legs.

'Okay,' said the boy. 'Do it!'

A bright white light flashed from within the machine, blinding Tark.

6: Administrators

Robbie led Zyra into another sterile white room. This one had a white table with three people seated behind it. The woman in the centre wore a dark blue suit, her peach-coloured lipstick matching the colour of her tie. Her dyed black hair was short and spiky. The woman to her left also wore a blue suit, but of a lighter shade, with her hair and makeup mimicking that of the other woman. The man wore a white lab coat, with a pale blue jumpsuit beneath. All three were intently studying computer tablets, their fingers brushing the surfaces and scrolling through information.

Robbie pointed to a lone white chair positioned a metre in front of the table.

Zyra raised an eyebrow but remained where she was.

'Sit,' said the woman in the centre, indicating the chair, her attention never leaving her tablet.

The other woman stifled a yawn.

Zyra cleared her throat loudly before striding forward to sit purposefully in the chair, her feet placed firmly on the floor in front of her – ready to leap up at a moment's notice. It was only once she was in the chair that she realised it was quite low, forcing her to look up towards the people behind the desk. From her position, Zyra saw that the desk was quite high, the people behind it seated on stools, their feet well off the floor.

Robbie positioned himself behind her right shoulder.

The woman in the centre continued working on her computer tablet, fingers tapping away. The other two now placed their tablets on the table and stared at Zyra, eyes not betraying any emotion. They both looked rather tired.

'Where's Tark?' asked Zyra, deciding to jump in and start the conversation. 'I want to see him.'

The woman in the centre held up a single finger as an indication for Zyra to stop talking.

Zyra huffed and crossed her arms.

The woman placed the tablet flat onto the surface of the table and looked down at Zyra. She pursed her peachy lips.

'We are the Administrators,' she announced as if expecting a standing ovation. Her voice was loud and precise. 'I am the Chief Administrator.'

The woman to her left spoke next, her manner and inflection a carbon copy of her superior. 'I am

Second Administrator Dorien.'

The man, by contrast, spoke softly and slowly, although his eyes never lost their hard edge. 'And I am Third Administrator and Designer-in-training, Welbourne.'

Zyra noted that he appeared a lot younger than the other administrators. They were, Zyra guessed, somewhere in their thirties or forties, while he couldn't be more than twenty-five.

There was silence as the three of them continued to look at Zyra with inscrutable gazes.

Zyra tightened her arms in front of herself. 'Well, my name –'

The Chief Administrator cut her off with another raised finger. 'We are well aware of who you are,' she said. 'The question is – what is to be done with you?'

Administrator Welbourne shifted his gaze from Zyra to Robbie. 'The scans indicate that the clone body is functioning correctly. You, robot, have interacted with her directly. Report.'

Zyra couldn't help noticing the way he said the word *robot*, as if it were some kind of insult.

'Zyra appears to be adapting well to her new body,' said Robbie, glancing briefly at her. 'She has accepted her existence in the real world. She is naturally curious about the situation that she finds herself in and wants to learn more. I believe that the more information she is provided with, the better her continued adaptation will be.'

Administrator Welbourne made some notes on his tablet.

'She is quite concerned about her partner, Tark,' continued Robbie.

Welbourne looked up sharply.

'It would be of great benefit to her emotional wellbeing if she were allowed to see Tark.' Robbie looked intently at the Administrators. 'They have an emotional attachment. And her emotional wellbeing is as important as her physical and intellectual wellbeing.'

'That will not be possible,' said the Chief Administrator.

'What do you mean?' asked Zyra, uncrossing her arms.

'You cannot see Tark,' said the Administrator sharply, as if that explained everything.

'Why not?' demanded Zyra, jumping to her feet.

Robbie put a calming hand on her shoulder.

'You cannot see him,' said the Chief Administrator, 'because he is not here.'

'But –' began Zyra.

The Chief Administrator raised a finger. 'He has been abducted.'

'What?' Every muscle in Zyra's body tensed.

'A group of adolescents managed to breach security and abduct the other clone,' explained the Chief Administrator. 'They also apparently intended to abduct you, but were unsuccessful. They seemed to know exactly where to find the other, but had trouble locating you. By the time they did discover your location, it was too late and security was able to intercept them. One of their number was captured.'

'She has been questioned,' added the Second Administrator, 'but has thus far proved uncooperative.'

'We are digressing,' announced the Chief Administrator. She indicated the chair to Zyra. 'Sit!'

Zyra's nostrils flared.

'You're telling me that Tark has been kidnapped,' said Zyra. 'Well, what are we going to do about it?'

'*You* are not going to do anything,' said the Chief Administrator. 'The other clone's abduction will be handled by security.'

'Would you stop calling us clones,' shouted Zyra. 'We are people! We have names!'

'Zyra,' said the Chief Administrator, pointedly. 'Sit!'

Zyra clenched her fists.

'Please,' said Robbie, gently, his hand on her shoulder again. 'Not now.'

Zyra hesitated a moment, then sat.

'There is still the matter of this clone to decide.' The Chief Administrator looked from one colleague to the next.

'She needs to be studied,' said Administrator Welbourne, eyes lighting up as he absently bit his lower lip. 'We could discover much from so perfect a specimen.'

'She is dangerous,' said Administrator Dorien. 'She should be placed in stasis.'

'That would not be ideal,' said Administrator Welbourne. 'It would be so much better if she were conscious.'

'Confinement, then.' Administrator Dorien looked pointedly across at her colleague.

'I am not some lab rat,' Zyra blurted out.

The Chief Administrator went to raise her finger again.

'Oh would you stop doing that,' said Zyra, springing to her feet. 'It's very annoying and extremely rude.'

'If I may be permitted to pass on a suggestion,' said Robbie, stepping forward to stand beside Zyra.

The Administrators all looked to him with a mixture of surprise and annoyance.

'It is the opinion of Designer Prime that Zyra should not be confined,' said Robbie, not waiting for the Administrators to respond. 'Designer Prime believes that it is important for her to interact with her surroundings. Designer Prime proposes that she be allowed the freedom of this research facility.'

'Ridiculous,' said Administrator Dorien.

'Interesting proposition,' said Administrator Welbourne. Dorien immediately glared at him.

'Impossible,' said the Chief Administrator. 'The research facility has far too many sensitive areas and –'

'Designer Prime is quite insistent,' interjected

Robbie. 'Designer Prime is willing to accept responsibility for her actions and offers my services as her guide to ensure her actions and movements remain appropriate.'

Zyra noticed the hint of a smile on Administrator Welbourne's face, before it disappeared.

'Very well,' conceded the Chief Administrator, obviously far from happy with the situation. She got to her feet. 'My objections will be noted in my report to Designer Alpha. This interview is now over.'

The other two administrators also got to their feet. A door opened in the wall behind them and all three left.

'What just happened?' asked Zyra.

'A minor power struggle,' said Robbie, thoughtfully.

7: Josie and the Rebels

As the light faded, Tark opened his eyes. Bright spots danced in his vision, obscuring everything. They diminished and a blurry form took shape.

Messy dark hair, golden brown skin, soft hazel eyes and full lips.

Tark smiled.

'So, you are awake,' said the beautiful face.

Tark suddenly remembered what had been going on. He sprang into a sitting position and almost fell off the table in surprise. Just a short while ago he could barely move a muscle, and here he was sitting up.

'You seem to be recovering quite nicely,' said the girl. 'My name is Josie.'

Josie was short. She was dressed simply in grey cargo pants and black, long-sleeved T-shirt. She was arrestingly beautiful.

'Oh ... ah ... I is Tark.'

'You *is* Tark?' Josie smirked. 'Don't you learn how

to talk properly inside the Game?'

'There ain't nuthin' wrong with the way I is talking,' said Tark defensively.

'Really?' Josie sounded less than impressed. 'Well, maybe not where you come from. But out here you're going to stick out like a sore thumb if you keep speaking like that. And believe me, you don't want to draw attention to yourself.'

The boy who had been giving orders earlier walked into the room carrying a computer tablet. Tark looked around, taking in his surroundings for the first time. The room looked like a cross between a storeroom and a makeshift laboratory. All sorts of medical equipment was sandwiched between crates and boxes. The windows had been covered over with black plastic and masking tape. The whole place had a worn-out ambiance.

'Got the results, boss,' said the boy.

'Well?' asked Josie. 'Spit it out, Devon.'

'He's perfect!' Devon handed the tablet to Josie.

Josie looked at the information on the screen, then back at Tark, arching one eyebrow. 'Perfect, huh?'

Tark suddenly felt vulnerable under her gaze. And cold.

'I is naked!' he announced, surprised.

'Yes,' agreed Josie, looking him up and down. 'Yes you are. You have an amazing talent for stating the obvious.'

Tark's hands shot out in front of himself, trying to

cover up the bits he didn't really want out on public display.

'Ah … I needs ta have clothes.'

'Sure thing.' Josie looked to Devon.

He sighed and went to rummage through a box in the corner of the room. He returned with an old lab coat covered with mysterious technicolour stains. Tark jumped down from the table, snatched the coat from Devon's hand and hurriedly put it on.

'Better?' asked Josie.

'It'll do.' Tark looked down at himself. The coat was too small. The sleeves were short on him, it barely reached mid-thigh level and the top buttons strained around his chest.

'Very good,' said Josie. 'Now, can we get down to business? There's a lot to fill you in on.'

'Yeah,' agreed Tark, eyeing Josie suspiciously. 'How comes I is not looking like I is supposed ta? Where is Zyra? Dids we gets outta the Game?' He took a step towards Josie, towering over her. 'And what the hell is you up ta?'

8: Designer Prime

The door slid open and Robbie ushered Zyra into yet another white room.

Unlike all the other rooms, this one was cluttered with an eclectic assortment of technology and furniture. For the first time since her arrival in the real world, Zyra felt a sense of individuality around her.

Two of the walls were lined with floor-to-ceiling bookshelves, dark and wooden, overflowing with dusty tomes. A third wall was lined with monitors, keyboards and goodness-knows-what-else. The wall of tech, thought Zyra.

The white of the floor was partly obscured by a large rug, the concentric patterns of a mandala woven through with muted reds and golds. A dark leather wingback chair stood slightly off centre, a small wooden table beside it. There was a glass of water and something that looked like a foil-wrapped food bar on the table.

Zyra looked back over her shoulder as the door slid closed behind her, disappearing into the wall. It was a bare white wall except for one framed painting to the left of where the door had been. Zyra stared at it.

An elderly, bearded man in white robes reclined on a cloud, his hand extended towards a computer monitor on the ground below. The naked man on the monitor reached up, his hand extending beyond the boundaries of the screen. Their fingers almost touched.

'It's called *Creation*.'

The voice was crackly and dry with an electronic edge. Zyra whirled around.

Something was detaching itself from the wall. A man emerged from the midst of all the technology, gliding forward in a contraption that was part chair and part life support system.

He was dressed in a jumpsuit. But his was different from those worn by others. It was a pink-flesh colour and it extended into a hood, encasing his head – his wrinkled face protruding like a dried prune through the oval in the fabric. Silvery strands of wiring were woven into the fabric, giving the jumpsuit a shimmering quality as it moved under the light. The man's waist and legs were totally encased by the chair. His left arm had a mechanical exoskeleton, pistons and cables simulating the movement of the muscles and tendons that no longer worked. His head was held back into a headrest by clamps, pierced by tubes filled with fluids.

The chair silently stopped in front of Zyra and Robbie.

'May I introduce Designer Prime.' Zyra thought she detected a note of awe in Robbie's voice.

The headrest turned slightly, moving the Designer's head so that his watery eyes fixed onto Zyra. They were a faded blue and looked oh-so-tired – and yet there was a spark of excitement buried deep within.

Zyra and the Designer regarded each other. The silence stretched as each of them considered the significance of this first meeting.

'Robert Vandenburg the Fifth.' The man did not move his lips. There was a vibration in his throat and his prominent Adam's apple bobbed up and down spasmodically, but the voice came from a speaker embedded into the surrounds of the chair.

'You is the ... I mean ... um ... you're ...' Zyra couldn't get the words to form.

'Yes,' said Robert. 'I am your creator.' He swallowed hard. 'And you are ... the meeting of two worlds. The digital made flesh and blood. My Game become reality. My ... virtual child.'

Zyra had a momentary urge to fall to her knees, but stopped herself. 'You are ... ah ... you're so ...' And still her thoughts couldn't transfer themselves to words.

'Old? Frail? Pathetic?' said Robert, his voice

betraying no emotion. 'Yes. I am. Do have a seat.'

He glided back and Robbie indicated the leather wingback chair. Zyra stared at it but did not move.

'You can sit down,' whispered Robbie.

Zyra plonked herself down into the leather. It creaked as if it had never been worn in.

'Please, have some water and food,' said Robert. 'You must be thirsty and hungry.'

Zyra tentatively picked up the glass of water and sniffed it.

'It is perfectly safe,' assured Robert.

Zyra took a little sip, swirled it around in her mouth, and then drained the glass. She hadn't realised just how thirsty she was. She was now also aware of how hungry she was. She picked up the food bar and tore open the wrapper. It was an unappealing grey bar. She sniffed and wrinkled her nose.

'It is a high protein bar,' said Robbie. 'It is exactly what your clone body requires.'

Zyra nibbled the end of it. The taste was plain, almost non-existent, and the texture was gluggy and chewy. Not at all pleasant. She ate it anyway.

'I realise that this is probably rather overwhelming for you,' said Robbie. She nodded while she chewed.

'Well,' said Robert, gliding up to Zyra. 'You must have questions.'

Zyra stared at him and the technology that surrounded him. He seemed more machine than man. She noticed that his chair did not touch the ground. It hovered a few centimetres in the air.

She finished chewing and swallowed the last of the protein bar.

'Questions.' Zyra nodded slowly, trying to collect her thoughts. 'Yes, I have questions.' Then she fell silent.

'Allow me to get you started,' said Robert. 'Question: Where is Tark? Answer: I do not know. Question: Can I help you get him back? Answer: No. Question: Are you a prisoner here? Answer: Officially, no. Technically, yes. Question: Are you in any danger? Answer: Not from me or Robbie. Question: What is this place? Answer: The Design Institute, although I used to refer to it as Designers Paradise. It is an independent research establishment and its purpose is the continued operation and development of the Game. Question: Who is in charge here? Answer: Officially, Designer Prime. In reality, Designer Alpha. Question: Who are the Administrators? Answer: Bureaucratic, but otherwise insignificant, pains in the neck. Question: How –'

'Stop!' cried Zyra, jumping to her feet and holding her hands up to her head. 'Enough already.'

Zyra thought she noticed a hint of a smile cross Designer Prime's wrinkled face, but it didn't linger.

'The Game,' said Zyra. 'Start with that. Tell me about the Game. What is it?'

'A good question,' answered Robert. 'I approve. Please sit down and I will do my utmost to give you an adequate answer.'

Zyra stared at him warily and sat down, the leather again creaking beneath her.

'The Game, as it now stands, is many things to many people.'

Zyra sighed theatrically and rolled her eyes.

'Patience is a virtue,' stated Robert. 'But its absence is not surprising given your virtual environment of constant adventure and danger.'

Zyra sniffed.

'When I first developed the Game it was simply an exercise in creation.' Robert glanced towards the painting on the wall. 'I have an interest. In fact, I have studied creation myths from across the globe.' He paused. 'There seemed, to me, to be an element of amusement in most of them. As if life, death, everything was for the entertainment of the specific deity or deities.

'It struck me that perhaps that's all that life was … a game. A game for the amusement of its creator. I liked the concept. I decided I wanted to be more than an amusement. I wanted to create. I wanted to be amused.' He smiled. 'I like games.'

'What?' Zyra looked a little bemused.

'I was not content to be a mere player in the game of life. I am a creator… a Designer … a …'

'A god,' finished Zyra. 'You think you're some sort of god.'

'To the inhabitants of the Game, I am.'

'You sound crazy,' said Zyra defiantly. She put more force into her words than she felt. Was she the crazy one, speaking like this to a Designer? But she felt an urge to exert her defiance. 'Crazy!'

'Explanations are going to take a very long time if you keep interrupting,' said Robert.

Zyra glared at him.

'Perhaps there is an easier way for this history lesson.' Robert looked at Robbie.

The robot fetched a headset from the wall of tech. He went to put it onto Zyra but she held up an arm defensively.

'It will not harm you,' explained Robbie. 'It is merely an information transfer device. Rather than Designer Prime telling you of events, with this you will be able to see them.'

Zyra lowered her hand cautiously, allowing Robbie to place the device onto her head. Little padded electrodes pressed gently onto her temples. They felt warm.

'Okay,' said Robert. 'Here we go.'

Zyra was no longer seated in Designer Prime's room. She was standing in large open area with rows of desks. Each of the desks had a computer workstation and each workstation had a person manipulating holographic displays with a virtual reality data-glove.

'The birth of the Game.' Robert's voice was all around her. 'Dozens of programmers creating code to my specifications.'

'Where am I?' asked Zyra, looking around, trying to find Robert. 'Am I back in the Game?'

'No, no,' said Robert. 'Getting into the Game isn't that easy. This is just a standard computer simulation based on my memories stored in a private database. You are hooked into it via the headset you're wearing.'

'Oh.'

'You will, no doubt, notice that it does not feel as real as the Game,' said Robert, appearing before her in his chair. Zyra did a double take. 'No smell, for starters,' he continued. 'And you can only observe. You can't touch anything.'

Zyra reached out to the desk in front of her. Her hand passed through it with a blur of pixels. She tried again. It was like disturbing an image reflected in water.

'And if you look closely, many of the details are indistinct. The failings of memory. The computer cannot simulate what I cannot remember.'

Zyra looked at the windows, but couldn't make out what was outside. It was just an indistinct mesh of blues and greens. She looked back to the desks and the people working at the computers.

'Their faces,' said Zyra with a sharp intake of

breath. 'I can't make out their features. They all look the same.'

'I don't remember all the people who worked for me,' Robert explained. 'People were not important to me.'

Zyra walked between the rows of desks, looking from one indistinct face to the next. She stopped suddenly.

'That's me,' she said in a startled voice. 'I mean it's Tina. Tina Burrows. The avatar that I used in the Suburbia environment.'

'Ah yes,' said Robert, gliding through the people and desks. 'Designer Burrows. I remember *her* very well.'

'What?' Zyra looked closely at the face. It was definitely Tina Burrows, although she was older than the avatar that Zyra had used. This Tina looked in her early twenties.

'Of course, she wasn't a Designer back then. Merely a rather promising PhD student with a talent for programming.' Robert moved forward, passing through the memory of Tina Burrows and along the row of programmers. The images pixelated and scattered as he went, reforming behind him. 'Follow me.'

Zyra followed, making a point of walking between the rows of programmers. Robert came to a stop in front of another desk. A familiar young man sat at this workstation.

'John Hayes,' breathed Zyra. 'Tark's Suburbia avatar.'

'He too would go on to become a Designer.'

'Why do our avatars look like them?' asked Zyra.

'Leftover memories.' Robert glided through John Hayes.

'What do you mean?' Zyra chased after him.

Robert finally came to the end of the row of programmers. He turned to face Zyra.

'You and Tark are far more linked to Designers Burrows and Hayes than you know.' He smiled. 'They were the first players … well, after me. They played as you and Tark. And they programmed the Suburbia environment.'

'They played as us?' Zyra felt her knees wobble.

'Yes,' said Robert. 'In the beginning, none of the characters had any consciousness, or even personality. They were merely avatars for real people to use. Of course, that changed over time. We introduced more sophisticated programming. Each character was given traits and purpose and the ability to develop a distinct personality.'

A series of images floated around Zyra. Tark and her on various adventures – fighting dragons, stealing money and striving to reach Designers Paradise. The two of them choosing their Suburbia avatars. Tina and John in Suburbia.

'Designers Burrows and Hayes introduced the Suburbia environment.' Robert's voice washed over the images like a documentary narration. 'It was the first additional environment. Hundreds more have since been added.'

The images continued. Vistas of many varied landscapes and cityscapes and bizarre places that defied description. And then Tina and John at workstations, programming. Tina and John in lab coats, watching others do programming. Tina and John in meetings with people in suits. Tina and John talking with another man in a lab coat.

Zyra looked closely at the man. He was tall, with brown curly hair and handsome features. There was a hint of grey at his temples, and the beginning of wrinkles at the corners of his blue eyes. He looked sad.

'That's you,' whispered Zyra.

'Yes,' Robert confirmed. 'That's me. Forty-two years ago. I was fifty, although I think I looked pretty good for my age. Tina and John were Designers by this stage. Had been for a while. Designers Burrows and Hayes. My best students. My closest collaborators. My greatest rivals.'

The memories of Tina and Robert began to argue.

'That was the day that everything changed,' said Robert. 'That was the day my focus shifted from creation to … I don't know … self-delusion.'

'What do you mean?' asked Zyra.

'Listen to them,' said Robert.

Zyra walked closer to the image from the past.

'You can't just abandon the project.' Designer Burrows waved her arms about in frustration. 'You've put too much into this.'

'As have we,' added Designer Hayes.

'I'm not abandoning it,' said Robert. 'I'm simply changing the focus. A virtual playground for disabled people.'

'There are so many other potential uses,' said Designer Hayes.

'Recent revelations have focused my attention on to this one,' said Robert.

'We can't just stop all our other lines of research.' Designer Burrows was red in the face.

'I'm no longer interested in those,' said Robert. He continued quickly as Designers Burrows and Hayes opened their mouth to protest. 'You can proceed with them, if you wish. Do what you like. I will not stop you.'

Designers Burrows and Hayes exchanged meaningful glances.

'I figured that you would be happier without my interference anyway,' added Robert.

Zyra watched everything blur, pixelate and reform.

It was the same three people having a similar conversation. As with the previous scene, their location was unclear. The main difference was that Robert was in a wheelchair – not the sophisticated technology-laden one he currently occupied, but something a little more ordinary.

'You're stagnant,' said Designer Hayes.

'I'm happy,' countered Robert.

'Are you?' asked Designer Burrows. 'Really? You're happy enough in the Game, playing as a child. But that's all you're doing – playing. You're not living. What you should be aiming for is a complete transference of your consciousness from the physical environment to the virtual.'

'We can do it,' said Designer Hayes. 'If you stop playing and start working, we could achieve this. Imagine – leaving your crippled, physical self behind completely.'

'Freedom from the physical world,' added Designer Burrows.

'What do I do with this freedom once I have it?' asked Robert.

Zyra's eyes widened. 'That's what Bobby said. In the Game.' She looked at the present Robert as his past self blurred and pixelated. 'You're Bobby? The Ultimate Gamer? How?'

Robert exhaled loudly. 'Just watch.'

The pixels reformed into another similar scene. Robert's wheelchair was now closer to its current form, although not as much of his body was encased in the technology. Designers Hayes and Burrows now wore pale blue jumpsuits under their white lab coats and they looked older. Designer Burrows in particular. Her face had hardened and lined.

'I don't understand you,' said Designer Burrows.

'We now have the technology to allow you to live in a virtual environment, full-time.'

'No thanks to you,' Designer Hayes uttered under his breath, glaring at Robert.

Designer Burrows shot him a stern look and he bit his lip. 'Yet you continue to play games and cling to your existence in this world.'

'Look at you,' Designer Hayes cut in. 'You can't even move without assistance. It won't be long before you're a complete vegetable.'

'And what would happen to my body out here, if I were to follow your advice?' asked Robert.

'What do you mean?' There was suspicion in Designer Burrows' voice.

'I'm not as stupid as you seem to think I am,' he answered. 'I know what's going on. I know what you're up to. I don't participate in your *research*, but I do watch. I know how you keep all those environments from collapsing. I know what happens to all those poor people.'

Designers Burrows and Hayes exchanged worried looks.

'Don't be so concerned. I'm not going to try to stop you. In return, you need to leave me the hell alone. I don't care what you do so long as you don't interfere with me.'

'Very well,' said Designer Hayes, cautiously.

'Oh, and I believe your cloning experiments have been a success.' There was a glint of victory in Robert's eyes. 'Well, I need a clone to assist me in this world.'

Everything blurred and pixelated again – and Zyra was back in the present, Robbie gently removing her headset.

Zyra rubbed her eyes and tried to clear her thoughts. 'Let me get this straight. Your name's Robert. You're also Bobby in the Game. And you've got a robot clone named Robbie.'

'That is correct,' replied Robert.

'Arrogant,' Zyra muttered.

'Perhaps,' said Robert. 'They are both aspects of me. Bobby is me as a young boy. He is my escape from the physical world. As for Robbie – he is my eyes and ears, my leg and hands in this world. He is ... special.'

'Bobby is dead,' said Zyra. 'I saw him die.'

'Oh Zyra.' Robert sighed. 'Nothing in the Game is necessarily what it appears to be. Yes, Bobby died and I exited the Game. When I go back, I'll be Bobby again. I'm always Bobby.' Robert's eyes shifted from Zyra and he stared off into nothingness. 'I programmed my twelve-year-old self into the Game right at the beginning. I scanned my memories and reconstructed him. Youth is such a precious thing. The mind works so differently before the pressures of life and responsibility slowly squeeze the joy and wonder and playfulness from it. The young mind is more adept at making a link to the virtual world.

More accepting. More imaginative. A situation that the other Designers have exploited with staggering success and recklessness.'

Zyra snapped her fingers at Robert to get his attention. 'What's all that supposed to mean?'

Robbie crossed between the two of them and to a console at the wall of technology.

'The Administrators have finished questioning the captured rebel,' he announced. 'They have failed to get any information other than her name – Mel.'

'Perhaps you and Zyra should visit Mel,' suggested Robert.

'What's the point?' asked Zyra.

'You might get some information about Tark.'

9: People Who Don't Matter

'Okays, let me gets this straight.' Tark was sitting on the end of the table, still dressed in nothing but the ill-fitting lab coat, trying to come to grips with everything that Josie had just told him. 'Zyra and me gots outta tha Game. But we is clones. She's a prisoner of the Designers. But ya rescued me.'

'That pretty much sums it up,' said Josie.

'That's a lot ta takes in.'

'Yes,' agreed Josie. 'I imagine it is. Get used to it. There's still a lot more for you to take in.'

'Yeah,' agreed Tark. 'Like wot yar lot's all about?'

'I really think you should at least try to speak like everyone else.' Tark opened his mouth to protest, but she continued. 'If we are going to help you get Zyra, we need you to be able to blend in. Surely Zyra is worth the effort?'

'I'm not stupid, you know,' said Tark, the gutter speak dropping away. 'I can fit in if I need to. I've spent enough time in Suburbia to be able to speak just like you.' He paused, a little surprised at how *right* the speech pattern felt. It didn't matter – no one was going to tell him how he should be talking. 'But till I needs ta ... Why shoulds I?'

'Suit yourself.' Josie spun and walked to the centre of the room, stopping to turn back and spread her arms. 'This is our research laboratory.'

'Looks a bit like a storeroom,' Tark said, unimpressed.

'Beggars can't be choosers,' Josie snapped back. 'We've converted this run-down Community Youth Centre as best we can. We're not a big-bucks corporation like the Design Institute. We're just a bunch a kids doing what we can to stand up for what's right.'

'Bit full of yaself, isn't ya?'

Josie took a deep breath, clenching her hands, then let it out slowly.

'We are on the same side,' she finally said. 'We share a common enemy. The Designers.'

'I isn't on no one's side 'cepts mine and Zyra's.'

'This is so much bigger than just the two of you,' said Josie. 'Aside from all the Game entities that have gained sentience, but are stuck in the Game ... there are the people in this world that the Designers are kidnapping.'

'Kidnapping?'

'Yes,' said Josie, pleased that she had at last gotten Tark's attention. 'The Designers have been taking kids.'

'How? Who?' asked Tark.

'Orphans, street kids, runaways, slum-dwellers – people who won't be missed, except by other people who don't matter.' Josie paced up and down. 'You see, there are different rules for different types of people in the real world – just like in the Game.'

'So why does the Designers want ta steals kids?'

'We're not sure,' admitted Josie. 'All we know is that it has something to do with the Game. And that they are never heard from again. We are trying to find out what's going on. And we'd like your help.'

'Eh?' Tark looked bemused. 'Wots can I dos?'

'You can go back into the Game,' said Josie. 'You can help us to find out what's going on.'

Tark's eyes widened. 'I've only just gotten outs.'

'I know,' said Josie. 'I know it's a big ask. But before you refuse, please hear me out.'

'Okays. I is listening.'

'We have a contact in the Design Institute,' explained Josie. 'And he, or she, has been slowly feeding us information and supplies. We now have a way into the Game.' Josie paused to lick her lips. 'But we can't use it.'

'Ah-ha.' Tark stared at Josie.

'There is some sort of security program on the Game,' continued Josie. 'It won't let any of us in.'

'Wot makes ya think it will lets me in?'

'You've just come out of the Game.' Josie's voice rose a notch, the hope and excitement evident. 'You're from the Game originally. I'm willing to bet that you'll get in. I think the security program might recognise you and let you through.'

'And wots does I do once I is in there?'

'You don't have to do anything for the moment,' said Josie. 'We just need to know that you can get in … and out again. Piece of cake.'

'Ahhh.' Tark pointed at Josie. 'That's it, ain't it. Ya isn't sure I can gets out again, is ya?'

'Well,' admitted Josie, avoiding Tark's eyes. 'Theoretically, you should be able to get out again. The nanos we're going to use to put you in are programmed for a time-limited access of ten minutes. So once your time is up, you'll exit automatically.'

'Theoretically,' added Tark.

Josie met his gaze. 'You are our only option. We took a great risk getting you out of the Design Institute. We lost one of our own during the raid. You –'

'Ya reckons I owes ya,' interjected Tark. 'Well, I owes ya nuthin'.'

Josie's face fell, hope draining from it.

'But I'll thinks on it. Now, can I has sum food? I is starvin'.' Tark jumped down from the table. The too-short lab coat rode up and he grabbed at it. Tugging it down, he felt it rip at the back. 'And can I please has sum proper clothes?'

10: Mel

'So do you think she might be able to tell us what's happened to Tark?'

Zyra looked hopefully at Robbie, walking next to her along corridor after identical corridor. The featureless walls and even lighting made it almost impossible for Zyra to make any sense of where they were.

'I do not know,' answered Robbie, truthfully. 'We shall find out shortly.'

They turned a corner and Zyra saw a guard standing against the wall. He was tall and broad, with an impassive face. He wore a black jumpsuit with padding and armour – bullet-proof and able to absorb an energy burst, according to Robbie. He also had accoutrements – a thick black belt around his waist and double bandoleer crossing his chest. There were various devices and pouches attached to the criss-crossed fashion accessory. On his right hand he wore a thick black glove – a bit like a data-glove, but menacing. It was inlaid with silvery threads and reminded Zyra of the glove the Cracker had once used to attack her and Tark.

'Power-glove,' explained Robbie. 'The wearer can throw a concentrated charge of energy – mild enough to stun you, or strong enough to kill you.'

'Toys!' whispered Zyra. 'Could have used something like that back in the Game.'

'Indeed.' Robbie brought them to a halt in front of the guard. 'We have permission to interview the prisoner.'

The guard cocked his head to one side as if listening to a voice no one else could hear.

'The guards are all cloned from Designer Alpha's original recruit,' Robbie explained. 'He was strong, ruthless and had an unwavering loyalty. The clones also have communications implants.'

The guard stepped aside as a door slid open in the wall. Robbie led the way in, adding, 'Designer Prime refers to them as *grunts*.'

There was a table with two chairs just inside the door. Beyond that, a girl sat in what looked like a plastic armchair. Everything was white.

Robbie sat down in one of the chairs, and motioned for Zyra to do the same.

The girl's eyes widened when she saw Zyra, but she didn't move.

Zyra studied her intently. She seemed unremarkable in every way – medium height, medium build, mousey mid-brown hair, cut short. Her face was plain. Her clothes were ordinary — black pants, black long sleeved top. She wore no jewellery. Her eyes were the only notable thing about her. There was a burning intensity to them, despite the absolute stillness of her body.

Robbie began the proceedings. 'My name is Robbie and this is Zyra. We would like to talk with you.'

The girl made no response, her eyes still fixed on Zyra.

'I understand that you have already been questioned by the Administrators,' continued Robbie. 'And that your name is Mel.'

The girl finally moved her eyes to look at Robbie.

'We were hoping that you might be able to answer some questions,' he said.

Still no response from the girl.

'WHAT HAVE YOU DONE WITH TARK?' Zyra shouted.

The girl blinked and slowly shifted her gaze back to Zyra.

'What's wrong with her?' asked Zyra, her voice back to a normal level. 'She doesn't move. She doesn't talk. Can she even understand us? Is she stupid?'

'She can't move,' explained Robbie. 'She is in a restraining chair. She is held in place with a low-level force-field. It should be set so as to allow her to speak. And she can certainly hear us.'

Zyra returned her attention to Mel. 'Well hear this. If Tark has been hurt in any way, I will kill you. You got that? I *will* kill you – slowly and painfully.'

Mel blinked.

'So tell us what the hell you've done with Tark,' said Zyra.

Mel closed her eyes.

'Fine,' said Zyra, getting to her feet. 'If that's the way you want it.' She shoved the desk to one side and strode forward.

'Stop!' said Robbie.

Zyra ignored him and made a grab for Mel's throat. Her hand stopped millimetres from its target. Try as she might, she could not get her hand to close around the girl's throat.

Zyra gave up and tried to pull back instead. That didn't work either. Her hand was stuck, immobilised by the same force-field that held Mel in place.

'I warned you,' said Robbie, still seated at the other end of the room. 'You have triggered a security alert as well.'

'Tark is fine.' Mel's voice was a harsh whisper, barely audible.

Zyra gave up struggling and stared at her.

'We rescued him from this evil place,' hissed Mel. 'They steal people. Kids. Find out what happens to them.'

A door opened up behind Mel. A guard and a technician entered.

'You're special,' said Mel. 'Be careful.'

'This is not acceptable,' stated the technician in a bland voice.

He tapped at his computer tablet. Zyra's hand came free and she staggered back. Mel went limp in the chair, slumping forward.

'Don't trust any of them,' whispered Mel.

'I beg your pardon?' said the technician, leaning forward.

Mel sprang up, knocking the tablet from the technician's hand, and grabbed him around the throat. The guard immediately raised his arm, power-glove at the ready.

Zyra tensed, her hands automatically going for her knives … that weren't there.

Mel edged towards the door, keeping the technician between herself and the guard.

'Stop!' the guard demanded, his voice deep and gravelly.

Mel continued to move across the room.

Zyra looked from Mel to the guard and back to Mel. Their eyes met. Should she help Mel? If Mel escaped, she might be able to lead her to Tark.

Robbie's hand gently touched her shoulder.

There was a crackle of energy and the technician collapsed to the floor with a whimper, leaving Mel out in the open.

Mel froze, eyes wide.

The guard fired his power-glove again and Mel

was slammed back against the wall by the bolt of energy. Her unconscious body crumpled to the floor. The guard swiftly strode forward, picked her up and slung her over his shoulder. Then he marched out of the room.

The technician groaned and placed a hand to his throbbing head. Staggering to his feet he noticed Zyra and Robbie staring at him, and paused. As if greatly embarrassed by the events, he hurriedly picked up his tablet and rushed from the room.

'Interesting,' said Robbie thoughtfully.

'What is?' asked Zyra, as the door they had entered through reopened.

'What Mel said to you.'

Zyra's eyes locked onto Robbie. 'You heard?'

'I have exceptional hearing,' said Robbie.

***

'Everyone has their own agenda,' said Robbie, leading Zyra down the corridor. 'Mel is right. You should not trust anyone. Not completely, at any rate.'

'What about you?' asked Zyra.

'Would you like a tour?' Robbie ignored her question.

'Really?' said Zyra. 'I'm allowed?'

'I would not be permitted to show you everything,' admitted Robbie. 'But there is a reasonable amount that I can.'

'Can you show me the Game?' asked Zyra.

'What do you mean exactly?'

'Well ...' Zyra thought about it. 'The computer that it is on? Or the hard drive? Or whatever?'

'Yes,' agreed Robbie.

More corridors. Blank white walls with harsh overhead lighting. Zyra wondered how anyone could know where they were going.

Finally, Robbie placed his hand on a portion of wall and a door opened. He led the way in.

The first thing that struck Zyra was the humidity. It was like walking into a wall of moist heat and finding it difficult to breathe.

Robbie had brought her into a room with a pool – at least, that was her initial impression. It was a sunken vat, about five metres in diameter. It was filled with a green, gelatinous substance that churned and bubbled and frothed. Tubes and pipes and wiring fed into the 'pool', disappearing from view beneath the surface. They snaked around the rim of the pool and connected to the walls around it. Condensation collected on the walls and ceiling, and dripped.

Although the room was white like all the others, the lighting was subdued. And the green gelatinous substance glowed from within.

'What is this stuff?' asked Zyra.

'Billions upon billions of organic nanobots,' answered Robbie.

'What are they for?'

'They are the mainframe,' said Robbie. 'The

matrix of information. They are the storage and the operation. In essence, they are the Game.'

'So ...' Zyra stared into the pool. 'The Game is alive.'

'In a way,' said Robbie. 'The nanobots are organic. But they are not sentient.'

'So this is the Game data.' Zyra lifted a hand to her ear but there was no metal stud for her to play with. 'How do the Designers control it all?'

'Programming portals. I can show you one.'

He led the way to another room. It was smaller and it was empty.

Zyra scanned the room. 'There's nothing here.'

Robbie walked to the centre of the room. 'Activate portal.'

'Security scan,' announced a disembodied, androgynous voice.

Waves of green light flickered across Robbie's body.

'Identity confirmed,' said the voice. 'Welcome, Robbie. Level four portal access granted.'

Holographic controls materialised around Robbie. His hands moved across the circle of keyboards, and into the mid-air displays, manipulating data directly and rearranging code.

'It's like the Ultimate Gamer's interface,' breathed Zyra.

'I suppose it is,' agreed Robbie. 'This is Designer Prime's portal. It is the original one. Each of the other Designers has one as well. Designer Prime allows me to use his.'

His hands continued to fly across the holographic displays.

'What are you doing?' asked Zyra.

'Nothing of any importance,' said Robbie. 'I am writing the coding for a cloud formation in the shape of my face. It will appear in Suburbia at random times, for exactly three point four seconds at each manifestation before beginning to disperse.'

'Oh,' said Zyra. 'How creative of you.'

'It amuses me,' responded Robbie, his hands slowing down. 'Session complete. Deactivate portal.'

The holographic displays disappeared and they were again in an empty room.

'So,' said Zyra, watching Robbie carefully. 'You need amusing. Interesting for a robot clone.'

'Would you like to try using the portal?' asked Robbie.

'Me?' Zyra's voice betrayed her surprise. 'I don't know anything about coding or programming. I wouldn't know what to do.'

'You would not be able to do anything,' said Robbie. 'Designer Prime has simply arranged observer level access for you.'

'Um ... okay then.'

Robbie stepped aside to allow Zyra into the centre of the room. 'Activate portal.'

'Security scan,' announced the voice.

Zyra flinched as the waves of green light flickered across her body.

'Identity confirmed,' said the voice. 'Welcome, Zyra. Observer level access granted.'

A holographic display of tiny images encircled Zyra. It was like being in the middle of hundreds of mini television screens.

'This is the environment menu. Each image represents a Game environment,' explained Robbie. 'Simply touch the one you would like to observe.'

Zyra chose an image at random. The image enlarged and enveloped her. She found herself in a holographic jungle, wan light filtering down through a lush green canopy.

'Raise your arm and extend it to move forward,' instructed Robbie. 'Then point into whichever direction you want to go. Punch forward to increase speed. Pull back to reduce.'

Zyra extended her arm and moved through the undergrowth, passing through bushes and trees. Looking around, she saw animals in the undergrowth and in the branches – snakes, monkeys, lizards and birds. They were all moving around as if on fast forward.

'Why are the animals moving around so fast?' asked Zyra. 'I can hardly see them.'

'Time differential,' said Robbie. 'The time scale inside the Game is variable. It can be sped up or slowed down. Accelerated development can allow the Designers to observe decades of progress over the course of mere hours.'

'Oh.'

Zyra continued to move through the landscape.

'You can also move up and down,' said Robbie. 'When you've had enough, swipe your hand, as if you are karate chopping an opponent.'

'Are robots programmed to be funny?' asked Zyra.

Robbie did not answer.

Zyra karate chopped a tree and the jungle disappeared. She looked at the environment menu, searching through the myriad images.

'To your left, third from the bottom,' said Robbie.

'How did you know what I was looking for?' asked Zyra. She located and poked her finger at the World that had been her home.

'Lucky guess,' answered Robbie.

'You don't seem like a robot to me,' said Zyra, as the City loomed up around her. She jumped as a gang of mutants appeared out of nowhere and then disappeared again. She raised her arm and moved through the environment. It was mostly deserted. Only a few people flickered in and out of existence. Occasionally the City was plunged into darkness, only to return to daylight seconds later.

'It seems even faster here,' said Zyra. 'It's hard to follow anything at this speed.'

Robbie stepped forward and leaned into the display. A holographic keyboard materialised. He hit a few keys and stepped back. Everything slowed down to a normal pace.

'I've stabilised the time differential for you,' he explained.

Zyra continued to search through the City. It wasn't long before she found the basement hideout that she used to inhabit with Tark – currently inhabited by copies of them.

The basement was empty.

'Out questing, no doubt,' said Robbie.

Zyra swiped her hand as if she really did want to karate chop someone, and the holographic image disappeared.

'Deactivate portal,' she grunted.

She was again in an empty room with just a supposed robot clone for company.

'All very impressive,' said Zyra.

'We should return to Designer Prime.'

11: Food

Devon put a bowl and spoon onto the rickety trestle table. Tark sat down and winced. He was still wearing the ill-fitting, torn lab coat, but now he wore a pair of pink bike shorts underneath. They were also too tight. He pulled at the clinging lycra.

'Sorry about the clothes,' said Devon. 'I've sent Len to try and find you something better.'

Tark grunted and looked down at his food – if you could call it that. It was a grey mush that looked very unappetising indeed. He picked up the spoon and plunged it into the bowl.

'Wots is it?'

'It's a high protein, high carb energy food,' said Devon. 'It comes in powdered form and you mix it with water. And it's cheap.' He smiled. 'Better than it sounds. I mixed in some sugar and some powdered milk as well.'

Tark lifted the spoon to his mouth and tentatively gave it a try. It had the consistency of mud. But it was sweet. And now that he had put a little into his mouth, he realised how hungry he was.

'Nots bad,' he said, shovelling the slush into his mouth.

Devon sat down next to Tark.

'What's it like?' asked Devon. 'In the Game?'

Tark swallowed and looked over at the boy. There was a curiosity that verged on eagerness in his eyes.

'Dunno.' Tark shrugged. 'Dangerous. Um. It wuz … wells … everything. It wuz alls I knew. It wuz … just our lives, I guess.'

'Oh.' Devon nodded as if he understood.

Tark doubted that he did. He took another mouthful, chewed on the lumps and swallowed. He looked at Devon. 'So, why is ya doing all this?'

'The boss already explained,' he said. 'We don't like what the Designers are doing. We're rebelling.'

'Yeah, I gets that.' Tark lifted another spoonful to his mouth. 'But how'd ya gets involved?'

Devon put his elbows on the table and leant his head on his hands.

'I used to be out on the streets. Saw kids getting taken. Guys in white coats offering food and games and a place to live. Seemed too good to be true. I said no. They tried to take me anyway. So I ran and hid. Then Josie starts nosing around. Asking questions. She saved me.'

He shuddered. Tark thought that at this moment, he looked more like a scared kid than a rebel.

'She gave me a place to live. Here. And I've been helping her. I went back to the streets and found Len and Tara.'

Tark chewed thoughtfully.

'It's hard out on the streets,' said Devon. 'This is better. Here we've got a purpose, as well as a place to live.' He smiled. 'Rebels with a cause.'

Tark finished his food.

'Takes me back ta sees yar boss.'

Devon led Tark back to the makeshift lab.

Josie was sitting in a corner, staring at a computer tablet. She held it up so Tark could see the photo on the screen.

'Her name is Mel,' said Josie, sadly. 'She was captured during your rescue. If not for her –'

'Oh, enough with the guilts,' said Tark, striding up to Josie. 'I'll does it. But I is doing it 'cause I wanna fight the Designers. I is doing it 'cause I wants Zyra back.'

'I was hoping you'd come around.' Josie smiled. 'Devon?'

Devon rushed over to a small refrigerator and retrieved something. He handed it to Josie and stepped back. Josie held up a small needle and syringe. It was barely the length of her little finger. She flicked it with her index finger to force any bubbles of air to the top, then gave the plunger a little push. The air was expelled and a tiny drop of green liquid formed on the tip of the needle.

'Wot are ya gonna do with that?' asked Tark, voice a little shaky.

'Inject it into your eyeball,' said Josie matter-of-factly.

'Ya keeps that thing aways from me.' Tark backed away.

'I'm sorry,' said Josie. 'This is the only way. Hold still.' Tark continued to back up. 'Devon?'

Tark felt something being pressed into his back.

'Nots again.'

He felt the charge course through his body, his muscles convulsing in response. His vision blurred and his legs gave out. He felt someone catch him and lower him to the floor.

Tark tried to get up but couldn't move. A distorted face swam into view.

'I am sorry it had to be this way,' said Josie, holding up the syringe. 'It's not as bad as it looks. There are painkiller nanobots bonded to the needle. They should take effect within milliseconds.' She took a deep breath. 'Okay. Devon.'

Tark felt a hand firmly take hold of his forehead. Then there were fingers on his face, holding his left eye open, making it impossible for him to blink.

'Sorry,' whispered Devon.

Josie turned the syringe, aiming the needlepoint at Tark's eye. His vision was still blurred and he could not focus on it, which he realised was probably a blessing. But he knew that the needle was slowly inching towards him.

Pain shot through his eye, announcing the needle's entry, searing its way through his entire face and head. If he could have screamed, he would have.

It was all over before it had much of a chance to register. Tark realised that Josie was telling the truth about the painkillers.

His vision now clouded over with grey. Sizzling, sparkling, swirling grey static rushed towards him with a whooshing sound like an oncoming tornado.

12: The Game

'The Chief Administrator has just filed her report with Designer Alpha,' said Robert, as Zyra and Robbie returned. 'Won't be long before she'll want to see the Game entity in the clone body.'

'You keep mentioning this Designer Alpha,' said Zyra. 'Is there a Beta as well?'

'Not anymore,' said Robbie. 'Designer Alpha disposed of him.'

'So, how did the interrogation go?' Robert cut in.

'I didn't realise it was meant to be an interrogation,' answered Zyra, coming to stand behind the leather chair.

'Merely a convenience of terminology.' Robert glided from the tech wall over to Zyra. 'A pity the young rebel was not a little more communicative.'

Zyra raised an eyebrow. 'If you already knew the outcome, why ask?'

'Courtesy.'

'The tour was more productive,' Robbie interjected.

'Did you enjoy seeing into the Game?' asked Robert.

'Enjoy isn't the right word.' Zyra stared ahead. 'It was … interesting. It felt strange – seeing it but not actually being in it.'

'Do you miss it?' Robert seemed eager for an answer.

'No. Yes. Sort of.' Zyra furrowed her brow in confusion. 'I definitely don't want to be playing the Game, but … It's just that this world still feels so unreal.' She shook her head. 'It's silly. This is the real world. The Game wasn't real. Yet my memories of it feel more real than …' She spread out her arms. '… this!'

'Sometimes I feel like I'm just a character in a game,' said Robert. 'Like I'm the one being manipulated.'

Zyra raised an eyebrow. Robert stared at her for a moment, then lowered his eyes. 'Sometimes I have this notion that we are just one world within many. That this *reality* is merely a game within someone else's reality. That we are here to entertain and amuse.' He paused and looked up to meet Zyra's eyes again. 'Worlds within worlds within worlds within … ad infinitum. Perhaps all of creation is just a game. Games within games within games … ad infinitum.'

'So this isn't really reality?' Zyra looked confused.

'Who knows?' Robert sighed. 'What is reality anyway, aside from what we make of it?'

Zyra watched Robert, encased in his chair looking up at her. There was that twinkle in his eyes again. *He's playing*, she thought. *He's playing with me.*

'I think this world *is* real,' she finally said. 'You're just trying to confuse me … to play with my mind. I think there's something wrong with you. You're obsessed with playing games. You become Bobby to play games. But no, that's not enough for you – is it? Bobby then has to become someone else – the Fat Man or the Pinball Wizard or whoever – to play more games within games. Even out here you're playing. You've created yourself a robot to listen in on the other Designers. I think you're playing with them. And now my existence in this world, my need to find Tark, my desire to find out what's going on … it's all just another game for you to play.'

Zyra leaned down and brought her face right up to Robert's. 'I am not your plaything. I will not be drawn into your stupid games.'

She stared into Robert's unblinking eyes. And he stared back.

'Bravo,' he finally said. 'Bravo. You really do have strength of mind. More so than most *real* people.'

Zyra straightened up and stepped back.

'It's true,' he admitted. 'I do like playing games. And yes, you could say that I am playing against the other Designers. They want very different things from me.'

'Yeah?' said Zyra. 'Well, what do they want?'

'Oh, the usual,' said Robert. 'Money, power, control over others ... world domination.'

'World domination with a game?' asked Zyra.

'It's so much more than a game these days,' explained Robert.

'Tell me about it.'

'Well.' Robert took a deep, rattling breath. 'Things started out with a simple virtual reality interface – data glove and headset. Limited interaction. Then we tried direct input with the brain via electrical impulses, giving a much more real experience. But there were still limitations. The human brain could only handle the virtual reality connection for short periods of time – a few hours at most. Reaching its limit the brain would begin to reject the connection.'

'Full immersion came with the development of a nanobot interface.' Robert paused. 'Perhaps I should show you. Take a seat.'

Robbie fetched the headset and placed it on Zyra. Once again, she entered Robert's thoughts.

A person lay on what looked like a hospital bed. She was surrounded by computer equipment and connected to numerous intravenous drips and monitors.

'Organic nanobots are injected into the player. They travel to the brain and create a direct connection to the Game. The player's experience in the virtual world is indistinguishable from reality. Because the brain accepts the experience as reality, there is no limit on the time spent in the Game. So long as the body is supplied with intravenous nutrients and muscles are kept toned with electrical impulses, the player could, theoretically, spend their entire life within the Game.'

The scene changed.

'Designer Burrows saw the potential in this for government contracts. Firstly in the area of military training.'

Zyra saw what appeared to be a large hospital room. Rows and rows of beds with unconscious bodies, all hooked up to the Game. People in lab coats walked between the beds, checking on the unconscious people and making notes on their computer tablets.

'War zone environments were created to train soldiers. It proved to be an effective method of training – low risk but high experience.'

The scene changed. It was now a much larger room, with a great many more people crammed in together. The room was darker and there was an air of abandonment. No one was checking on these people.

'With skyrocketing prison costs, the Department of Corrections funded a trial program. Criminals were placed into the Game. They were punished by being given characters and situations that placed them as victims. Robbers became those being robbed. Corporate criminals who embezzled large sums of money to finance extravagant lifestyles found themselves in unimaginable poverty. Those who committed violent crimes were forced to be the victims of violent crimes. Murderers got to experience being murdered ... the fear, the helplessness, the pain ... over and over again.'

'That's horrible!' said Zyra.

'Yes, I suppose it is,' agreed Robert.

The scene shifted.

More unconscious bodies. Hundreds of them were suspended in fluid filled bags, connected by tubes to bubbling vats of nanobots.

'Clones,' said Robert. 'The Designers have been growing them. Perfect versions of themselves.'

Zyra realised that all the bodies looked the same. They all looked like her ... like Tina Burrows. But not quite like the real Tina Burrows. These clones were idealised versions of her with perfect, toned musculature and flawless beauty.

Zyra took a closer look at one of them, crouching down and bringing her face right up close to its womb-like bag. The clone's eyes were shut, its face slack. Its skin was tinged green by the surrounding fluid. It was not breathing, so there was no movement. It looked eerily embryonic and corpse-like at the same time. Zyra shuddered and straightened up. This is what her clone body had looked like before her mind had been downloaded.

Zyra hurriedly moved through the bodies, eager to

move on. At the end of the room she passed through the wall into an identical room. This one was full of faultless John Hayeses.

'If I look like Tina … is this what Tark now looks like?'

'Yes,' answered Robert.

Zyra looked into of the bags. Her eyes appreciatively scanned along the toned muscles and perfect skin. She tried imagining Tark in that body and the corners of her mouth curled up involuntarily.

'These bodies are ready to have Game entities downloaded into them.'

'Like Tark and me?'

'Yes and no,' said Robert. 'Game entities – yes. But not independent, freethinking entities that have become their own people. Game entities that have been programmed and trained by the Designers.'

'Why?' asked Zyra.

'Remember I mentioned world domination,' said Robert. 'Designer Burrows is up to something big. Her ambition has grown over the years. But I do not know to what extent. Thankfully, she has not yet succeeded in a download. You and Tark have the distinction of being the only two successful downloads.'

'Tark is in the Game!' Robbie's voice cut through the virtual image.

13: Desert Sands

Tark suddenly felt hot.

He squinted as his eyes tried to adjust to the brightness. He held up a hand to shade his face and looked out over an endless expanse of sand. Twin suns shone down from a lavender-hued sky.

'Greats!' said Tark, his mouth immediately feeling dry and dusty.

He slowly turned 360 degrees, eyes scanning the horizon. Nothing but sand as far as he could see, flat and featureless in one direction, dunes rising up in the other. He was beginning to sweat, his clothes feeling heavy and making him hotter.

Clothes?

He looked down at himself. Leggings. Boots. Tunic. Cloak. He was back in his old outfit. Tark lifted a hand, running his fingers along the scar that cut a path through the stubble on his head.

'I is me again,' he whispered.

'You're in!' Josie's excited voice rang in his head.

Tark whirled around. She was nowhere to be seen.

'Where the hell is ya?' he growled. 'When I gets me hands on ya, I is gonna makes ya sorry.'

'I'm not in there with you,' said her disembodied voice. 'There were some communications nanos in the mix. I'm still in the laboratory with your body.'

Tark clenched his fists and snarled.

'It's just a vocal communication,' she continued. 'Can you tell us where you are?'

'I is in a desert,' he said flatly.

'What can you see?'

'Sand!'

'Anything else? Can you see any signs of life?'

'No,' said Tark, looking around again. 'It don't matter anyways. Zyra and me brokes the rules. We can't interacts with anyone.'

'We're not certain of that,' said Josie. 'You've exited the Game and now re-entered as a player. Remember, you're not a Game entity any more. You're a real person, playing the Game. I'd say there is a pretty good chance that you'll be able to interact and play.'

'Well, there ain't anyone here to play with!' shouted Tark.

'Change environments.'

'How?'

'You've just got to think it,' explained Josie.

Tark was just about to tell Josie where he would like her to go, when he caught a glimpse of something – a flash of light on the horizon. He again held up his hand to shield his face from the harsh sunlight. Far off in the distance, something was moving. Coming closer.

'I sees sumthin',' he announced. 'Sumthin' moving across the sand. It's coming towards me.'

'Excellent!'

Tark watched as the shape came into view. It was a huge ship with sails and masts, skimming across the sand at an incredible speed.

'It's some kinda ship.'

A cloud of smoke burst from the oncoming ship, followed a second later by a booming sound. Shielding his eyes, Tark saw a black dot sailing through the air. And it was getting bigger. He turned to run. The ground a dozen metres to the right of him erupted in a geyser of sand.

Tark threw himself to the sand, shouting, 'They is shooting ats me!'

'Excellent!' cried Josie, her voice going up a notch. 'They must be able to see you then.'

'No kiddin'!'

'So you can probably interact and play,' added Josie.

'I don'ts care!' yelled Tark. 'Gets me out!'

'We can't,' said Josie. 'Sorry! It's time limited. You're stuck in there for another seven minutes. You've got to change environments ... or RUN!'

Tark struggled to his feet and took off as fast as

he could – which wasn't all that fast, as his feet kept sinking in the soft sand.

BOOM!

The ship fired again. Another cannonball came hurtling towards Tark. He heard it strike the ground behind him.

'I needs a gun!' Tark screamed.

He ground to a halt as a holographic display popped up in front of him. Images of firearms floated in the air. Tark rubbed his hands together with glee and poked a finger at the image of a shoulder-mounted rocket launcher.

The image glowed red. Text appeared below it: *Access denied. Insufficient game points.*

'Not fair!' Tark looked at the smaller weapons.

BOOM!

Tark took off, running through the weapons display, the images dispersing. The cannonball hit the ground and he felt a spray of sand.

'Change environments,' he mumbled to himself, struggling on. 'Gotta gets away from 'ere,' he continued to mutter between breaths. 'Thinks of something. Not a desert. No sands.'

He risked a quick glance over his shoulder. The ship was much closer.

BOOM!

Tark put on an extra burst of speed. As the cannonball hit, he felt the ground shake. The force of the impact knocked him off his feet.

Tark tried to think about the absence of sand as he sailed through the air. The only image his mind could form was ... grass.

14: Into the Game

'Tark's in the Game? How? Why?' Zyra jumped up from the chair, ripping the headset off and tossing it to one side. She was back in Robert's room, the images created by the headset, gone.

'I cannot answer any of those questions.' Robbie was standing by the wall of tech, hands moving across holographic displays, with a speed and dexterity that reminded Zyra of the Ultimate Gamer.

'A downloaded Game entity re-entering the Game as a player,' mused Robert. 'I had considered the possibility, but …' His voice rose with excitement. 'Monitor it, Robbie. Record all the data.'

'Monitoring and recording,' said Robbie. 'He is in the War of the Sands environment.'

'What's that?' asked Zyra.

'Dangerous,' answered Robert, a hint of a smile on his lips. 'He may need help.'

'How do I get in?' Zyra stalked over to Robbie.

'It may be better if I handle this,' said Robbie.

Zyra wasn't convinced.

'I have got a link on Tark's vital signs,' Robbie announced. 'They're highly elevated.'

'What does that mean?' demanded Zyra.

'He's under stress.'

'Why?'

'He must be in trouble,' concluded Robert.

'Get me in there now,' demanded Zyra, striding up to Robbie. Then lowering her voice she added: 'Or I'll break every bone in your cloned body.'

Robbie stared at her, genuine surprise in his eyes. Then he glanced back at Designer Prime.

'Let her go,' said Robert, without any hesitation. 'You go as well to gather first hand data.'

Robbie's hands moved across holo-displays. 'I am programming two doses of user controlled nanobots. This will allow us to change environments if necessary and exit when ready.' He finished off with a flourish and took two syringes from a dispenser in the wall.

'What are those for?' asked Zyra.

'You need to inject the nanobots,' explained Robert. 'They are what will enable you to re-enter the Game.'

'You had better sit down,' suggested Robbie.

Zyra returned to the seat and Robbie approached her with the first syringe. He brought it up to her face and she held up her hand.

'What are you doing with that?'

'It needs to be injected into your eyeball,' said Robbie.

'You've gotta be kidding,' said Zyra.

'I did say that entering the Game was difficult,' said Robert. 'If we had more time, we could set up an IV. But we don't. So the nanobots must be injected as close to the brain as possible. Theoretically we could inject it up your nose. Or in your ear. But we find that the eyeball works rather well.' He paused. 'Do you still want to go in?'

'Yes!' Zyra snapped without hesitation, leaning back into the chair.

'Excellent!'

Trying desperately to calm herself, Zyra concentrated on not blinking. Robbie leaned forward, bringing the needle towards her left eye. She watched it blur out of focus.

'There are pain numbing nanobots,' said Robbie. 'Their effect is almost instantaneous.'

Pain exploded through her eye. And then disappeared.

The familiar grey static of the Interface rushed towards her and she was back in the Game.

15: Machines

Tark landed face first in a field of grass. He decided he didn't like the taste.

'Greats!' he grumbled, staggering to his feet.

The grass stretched out in front of him towards gently undulating hills in the distance.

'Where are you?' Josie's voice piped up.

'How in heck is I supposed to knows,' snapped Tark.

'Describe the environment,' ordered Josie.

'Green,' answered Tark. 'Lots and lots of grass.' He looked up. 'Dark grey cloudy sky.' He looked to either side, then behind. 'And trees. There is a forest behinds me. I is going to goes there. I knows forests.'

'No people around?'

'Yar not on about that again, are ya?' asked Tark. 'I was being shots at in the desert. I thinks that means I is able ta interact.'

'We need to be certain.'

'Damnit!' snapped Tark, looking off into the

distance. 'Here I goes again.'

'What is it?'

'There is some sorts of machine thing coming over them hills at me,' he explained. 'Big. Real big! Belchin' out lots of smoke.'

It looked like a giant city-sized tractor, with massive wheels and enormous smokestacks reaching up toward the clouds. Tark followed the billows of grey up to the sky with his eyes.

'They ain't clouds,' he whispered. 'The sky is all covered in smoke.'

'What was that?'

'Neva minds.' The loud, grinding sound of machinery brought his attention back down to earth. Tark looked back at the giant tractor-city. His eyes widened as he realised just how fast the contraption was travelling. 'I got to gets to the forest. Nows!'

Tark turned and ran. Grass, at least, was a lot easier to run through than sand. Behind him, he heard the grinding sound of machinery getting closer and closer.

'What's going on?' asked Josie.

'Not nows.'

'But –'

'Shuts ups,' Tark panted.

Reaching the safety of the trees, Tark stopped and looked around. The tractor-city was painfully grinding to a halt, steam expelling in gushes from exhaust pipes above the gargantuan wheels.

It was now close enough for Tark to see that it was indeed a city. Huge metal structures grew out from the tractor-like base. In the shadow of five enormous smokestacks, hundreds of smaller ones belched grey smoke and black soot into the air.

As Tark watched, an enormous drawbridge lowered from the hull. It crashed down onto the grass. Tark heard the clanging sound of metal on metal. It was like the sound of giant metal footsteps. And indeed it was.

A gargantuan metal man lumbered down the ramp, clanging with each step. It was a bit like a robot – and yet unlike any robot he had ever seen. It was box-like and cumbersome, with pistons and gears spewing steam with every movement. Its eyes were like searchlights and its mouth like a fiery hell, flames and smoke visible through the gigantic rectangular slot.

The metal man stepped off the ramp and came to a stop. The clanging continued ... as another metal monstrosity lumbered down the ramp. And another. And another.

Tark didn't wait around to see how many more there were. He ran!

The trees and undergrowth were not too thick and the ground was not overly rough. Tark found it easy going, so it was not long before complacency tripped him up and he landed flat on his face beside a particularly large and leafy tree. In the distance he heard the sound of metal men crashing through the forest. Muttering curses, he went to push himself up, when a booted foot planted itself on the raised tree root right in front of his nose.

It looked familiar. He lifted his eyes a little and saw a swish of red leather.

'Tripping over your own feet? Lucky I'm here to help you up.'

'Zyra!' Tark gasped.

Zyra extended her hand. Tark grabbed it and she pulled him to his feet. Seconds later, he had her in a tight embrace.

The crashing sounds grew nearer.

'Thank the Designers ya is okay,' he breathed, then kissed her.

'Don't thank the Designers,' Zyra spoke against his lips. 'They're not worth it.' And then she kissed him back.

'What's going on?' Josie's voice shouted in Tark's head.

'Not now,' Tark muttered.

'Huh?' Zyra pulled back from him, irritated.

'No, no,' said Tark. 'Nots ya.'

The sound of someone noisily clearing his throat made them spring apart.

'There is a time and a place for everything,' said Robbie, standing a few paces behind Zyra. 'But this is neither the time nor the place for that. My data indicates that there are several armies converging on this area. And it is only a matter of time before the security program tracks us down.'

'Who in heck is he?' asked Tark.

'Um ...' Zyra stared at Robbie. He had hair, arranged in a neat side part, eyebrows and lashes. 'That's Robbie. He's a robot clone.'

'How cans he be a robot and a clone?' asked Tark.

'Long story.'

The sound of trees being ripped apart announced the arrival of the first of the metal men. Tark, Zyra and Robbie looked up to see the mechanical man's chest plate swing open with a hiss of steam. The barrel of a gun extended out.

'Now that's a robot,' yelled Tark, grabbing Zyra and pulling her to the ground.

The gun boomed.

'We do not appear to be the target,' said Robbie, calmly.

Tark and Zyra looked up to see where Robbie was pointing. High up in the air a gigantic airship was manoeuvring through the smoke. The shell stuck the gondola. There was an explosion and then flames and smoke belched from one side.

The metal man's gun burst into life a second time. There was a massive *woof* of flame as the entire airship disappeared in a huge burst of heat. Flaming wreckage rained down into the trees around them.

'I really would advise vacating this environment,' said Robbie.

'How?' asked Zyra.

Fire spread through the trees while three more machine men crashed through the forest towards them. From the opposite direction they heard a mechanical droning sound, like a giant saw cutting through wood.

The first mechanical man's gun retracted, its chest plate swinging shut. It inclined its head, the beams from its searchlight eyes slicing through the accumulating smoke and focusing on Tark and Zyra. The two of them jumped to their feet.

'I wants a weapon,' announced Tark. 'Shows me wots I can has.'

A series of holographic images sprung up in front of him – several swords and a couple of knives.

Zyra caught on quickly. 'Available weapons!'

Tark and Zyra made their selections as the metal man lifted its arm and an enormous Gatling gun popped up from a concealed hatch.

Tark was now holding a sword and Zyra had two knives. They looked up into the barrel of the Gatling gun.

'I don't think they will be very effective,' said Robbie. 'Take my hands.'

Tark and Zyra dropped their weapons and each took hold of a hand. The Gatling gun fired, bullets ripping up the vacant ground.

***

Still holding Robbie's hands, Tark and Zyra stood in

a field of golden flowers, a blue-as-blue-can-be sky above them.

'One minute to exit.' Josie's disembodied voice rang in Tark's head. 'Are you safe?'

'I is fine,' said Tark, dropping Robbie's hand and looking around. 'Wot is this place?'

'I've been here before,' said Zyra, looking around.

'It's Bobby's thinking place,' said Robbie.

'Is Robert going to be joining us?' asked Zyra.

'No,' answered Robbie. 'When Designer Prime plays the Game, it is always as Bobby. I think he feels that Bobby would not necessarily be helpful right now.'

'Wot is going on?' demanded Tark. 'I thoughts Bobby was this Ultimate Gamer. And he's dead! Wot's he gots to do with all this?'

'It's a bit difficult to explain,' said Zyra. 'Yes, Bobby died. But he's Designer Prime in the outside world. So he could go into the Game and be Bobby again. He got us out of the Game.' Zyra paused for a moment to think. 'And this is Robbie. He's a clone of Designer Prime. But he looks different on the outside.'

'Fifteen seconds,' said Josie.

Zyra stared at Robbie. With hair and eyebrows and eyelashes, he didn't look weird at all. In fact, he was quite good looking. A younger version of Robert. An older version of Bobby.

Zyra smiled.

Robbie smiled back.

'Why the hell is ya still holding his hand?' Tark blurted out.

'Exit!' Josie's voice called out.

And Tark was gone.

'Tark! Why did you –' Zyra hurriedly let go of Robbie's hand. 'What about us? How do we get out?'

'Our nanobots were programmed for emergency exit,' said Robbie. 'We can exit at any time.' He looked thoughtful before continuing, as if he were trying to decide whether or not to make a revelation. 'You really must beware of the Designers. They are dangerous. And they play games with people's lives.'

'What about Robert?'

'He is Designer Prime.'

The flowers shifted,

'What was that?' asked Zyra.

'The security program has located us,' he said. 'It is time to exit.' He took her hand. 'Ask Robert about the missing children.'

And they were both gone.

16: Kiss

Tark's eyes snapped open. Josie was staring down at him, face close to his. On impulse, he took her face in his hands and kissed her.

It took her a moment to recover from the surprise and to pull back. She quickly jumped to her feet and stepped even further away, glaring at Tark.

Tark, muscles still a little sluggish in responding, slowly sat up and then stood. He sniffed and wiped his sleeve across his nose, then faced Josie and smiled.

Josie stepped forward …

And punched him in the nose.

It was not a particularly hard punch. But it did hurt. And it took Tark completely by surprise. He staggered but just managed to keep his footing. He put a hand to his face and wiped away a trickle of blood and a smear of green.

'Do that again and I'll …' Josie clenched her fist again, leaving the threat hanging.

'Wot?' demanded Tark. 'Sticks me in the eye with a needle?'

Josie unclenched her fist.

'Or zaps me so I can't move?' His jaw tightened. 'Or kidnap me?'

'If that's what you do when you're angry with someone ... what happens when you like them?' asked Josie.

Tark stared at her for a moment, then his face broke into a smile and he chuckled.

'I wuz confused,' he said, looking a little embarrassed. 'That's all.'

'Uh-ha,' said Josie, nodding. 'Fine. Let's forget it then.'

'Yeah,' agreed Tark. 'Forgets it.'

It was at that point that Tark realised that he had an audience. Devon, Len, Tara and a couple of other kids were standing to the side of the room, silently staring at him and Josie.

'Wot is ya looking at?' growled Tark.

The kids hastily dispersed, some leaving the room, others getting on with chores.

'Me eye aches,' said Tark, changing the subject. He rubbed at it. 'I thoughts ya said there wuz numbing thingies in that needle.'

Devon walked up to Josie. 'All good?'

Josie ran a hand through her unruly hair. 'Now that we know Tark can get into the Game we can move on to the next step.'

'And wots would that be?' Tark fumed. Josie and

Devon looked at each other and then at Tark.

'We need to send you back into the Game, of course,' said Josie. 'This time, with a purpose.'

'Greats!'

'Not straight away,' assured Josie. 'Go get some food and rest first.'

***

Tark was back at the trestle table with Devon, staring at another bowl of mush.

'I mixed some orange juice in this time,' said Devon.

'You're a real ... Ya is a real chef.'

Devon smirked.

'Wot?'

'It's not a natural way of speaking,' said Devon. 'Probably felt fine inside the Game, but now that you've got a real mouth and tongue that hasn't been programmed, it sounds like it's actually difficult for you to keep talking like that.'

Tark scowled and shoved a spoonful of mush into his mouth.

'It's kind of silly to keep talking like that if you've got to concentrate on it.'

'Got any ice-cream?' asked Tark.

'I wish.'

Tark dropped the spoon back into the mush.

'So what's with Josie?'

'She's our leader,' answered Devon. 'Our boss.

She got us all together. Got us organised. Found this place.'

'Yeah, but what's her angle? Why's she doing all this?'

'Her brother,' said Devon. 'She and her brother used to live in an orphanage. Then the Designers showed up, wanting kids. They did these tests, getting them all to play games. And they chose some of the kids. Took them. Josie's little brother Alex was one of them. And he –'

'Never came back!'

Tark and Devon turned to see Josie standing in the doorway.

'The official story was that he ran away,' continued Josie. 'I know that's not true. The Designers took him. And they did something to him. And I want to know what.' She walked over to the table. 'He wasn't the only one they took.' She pulled a chair out and sat down. 'Mel and I are pretty good with computers. So we started to do some snooping. Other orphanages had lost kids. And then there were the homeless kids who disappeared. And the runaways who were never found. Of course, the police don't care about them.'

'And you think the Designers have all these kids?' asked Tark.

'Yes. But the more we've investigated, the stranger things have become. When we hacked into the Design Institute computer system –'

'You broke into the Game?' Tark interrupted.

'No,' said Josie. 'That's a separate system. A biological system. I mean their regular computer network. When I hacked into that, someone at the Design Institute caught me. But they didn't turn me in. Instead, they helped me. Gave me info. Gave me tech info. Even sent some equipment. I mean, it's old equipment. Real old. Like it was destined for recycling or something. But we use it. That's how we've been able to make the nanos to get you into the Game.'

'So what's the big deal about getting me into the Game again?' asked Tark.

'Something is going on in there,' said Devon.

'There is a sealed off section,' explained Josie. 'A hidden environment. Even our informer doesn't know what's going on in there. But he thinks it's something bad. And it's connected to the missing kids.'

'What makes you think I can do anything?'

'I'm not sure that you can,' admitted Josie. 'But we'd really like you to try. Especially now that they have Mel.' She looked at Tark with a defiant stare. 'It may be too late for Alex. But I won't let them keep Mel. I will get her back.'

Tark nodded slowly. 'Does it have to be the eyeball?'

'Sorry.' Josie shrugged.

17: Children

'Is Tark all right?' asked Robert, as Zyra opened her eyes.

'Yes,' Zyra answered, rubbing her face and sitting up. 'He got out.'

She blinked. The left eye was a bit teary and felt sensitive.

'What was he doing in there?' asked Robert. 'And how did he get in?'

'The rebels put him in there,' said Zyra, rubbing at her eye. 'I'm not sure why.'

'He had time-limited nanobots and a communications link to the rebel leader,' Robbie explained further.

Zyra glanced at him. He was hairless again. After seeing him in the Game, it struck her just how weird his appearance was in the real world. He was standing by the dispenser, an empty syringe still in his hand. It occurred to Zyra that he must have injected the nanobot solution into his own eyeball. The thought made her shudder.

Robbie caught her staring at him and blushed. He quickly turned his attention to the wall of tech. Zyra wondered if robot clones were supposed to blush.

'How did they get the tech to do that?' Robert wondered.

'A good question,' said Robbie, taking a glass of water from the dispenser and passing it to Zyra.

Zyra took a sip of water and ran her unexpected Game experience through her mind.

'It felt different,' she finally said, 'being in the Game just then. I can't put it into words, but it felt different from when I was living in the Game.'

'Of course,' said Robert, as if it were the most logical thing in the world. 'You are no longer a Game entity. And you can never truly go back. You are now a player. It's very different.' He chuckled to himself. 'A Game entity who is now a player. Bravo.'

Zyra took another mouthful of water and considered this information. She sniffed, her nose feeling a little dribbly, and wiped at it with her hand. She was shocked to see a smear of green on her hand.

'A side effect of the injection,' said Robbie. 'There is a connection between the nasal cavity and the nasolacrimal duct in the eye. Excess liquid drains from –'

'Yeah, yeah, fine,' interrupted Zyra. 'I don't need

the details.' She then turned her attention back to Robert. 'Mel mentioned kids. She said I should find out what happens to them. And you play as a child version of yourself. What is it about the Game and children?'

Robert stared long and hard at Robbie, then turned his attention back to Zyra.

'Imagination! Playfulness! Creativity! Resourcefulness! The ability to adapt to new situations!' After the rapid-fire list, he paused. 'All these things converge in young people. Not too young, because then there is a lack of focus. Not too old either, when they start to question too much and realise responsibility. It's a difficult age to pinpoint. And it varies from child to child. For me it is twelve. That's how old Bobby is in the Game. For others it could be ten, or fifteen, or maybe even as old as seventeen. It depends on the individual. For some it can last years. Others have a much shorter period of usefulness.'

'Usefulness?' Zyra stood up, unease filtering into her movements. 'What do you mean?'

'Ah.' Robert's chair glided around so that he was facing the tech wall, away from Zyra. 'Usefulness is in the eye of the beholder. I found children useful in programming the Game. I scanned the brains of many children when creating the Game structure. Once it was there, I connected myself to the matrix and probed my own memories, accessed my twelve-year-old self. I used him – me – to shape the Game.' There was a long pause. 'And, of course, the Designers now use children to maintain the integrity of the environments.'

'What's that supposed to mean?'

'It means that there are children – dozens of them – connected to the Game, keeping the environments from collapsing.'

'I still don't get it,' said Zyra. 'How?'

'Perhaps it would best for you to see for yourself.' Robert's chair spun around so he could again look at Zyra. 'Robbie.'

Robbie slid open the door and stepped through it. 'I'll take you.'

Zyra drank the rest of her water and followed him.

'You won't like it,' Robert called after her.

Zyra paused in the doorway, not turning back to look at him. As she followed Robbie, she thought she heard Robert say, 'I don't like it, either.'

***

Zyra's eyes were wide with horror. Her mouth hung open and she tried to form words. But all she could do was stare.

Ahead of her were rows and rows of unconscious children. They were lying in hospital beds that were crowded together in a long room. Each one of them was hooked up to an intravenous drip of green, nanobot-laden liquid. There were banks of computer equipment, monitors and life-support apparatus.

They looked so much like terminal patients waiting to die.

'Are they all playing the Game?' asked Zyra, her voice a hoarse whisper.

'No,' replied Robbie. 'They are keeping it running. Providing the background brainpower to keep the rules in place and the environments separated. They are the glue that holds it all together. They are not in our world and they are not truly in the Game either. They are in a limbo. The necessary parts of their brains are stimulated with nanobots. Everything else is held in check. They may have a fleeting realisation of their non-existence, but as far as I can tell, there is no true consciousness either in this world or the Game.'

'And they're kept like this,' gasped Zyra, 'forever?'

'No,' said Robbie. 'Eventually their brains wear out.'

Zyra lifted a hand to her mouth and closed her eyes. 'This is horrible,' she whispered against her fingers.

'Yes,' agreed Robbie. 'It is.'

Zyra opened her eyes again. 'Why aren't they at least allowed to live in the Game?'

'It would be a waste of resources,' said Robbie. 'If they played, they would have less brainpower to be utilised for the Designers' purposes. And they wouldn't last as long. There is also the possibility that they might not cooperate.'

'Could they play?' asked Zyra. 'Could they be given different nanobots?'

'In theory,' conceded Robbie. 'I suppose it would be possible. But the Designers would never allow it.'

Zyra took a few steps closer to the first of the unconscious bodies. She gazed at the girl. Her breathing was so shallow, the plastic tube that fed into her mouth giving her just enough oxygen to keep her alive.

'Mel!' Zyra mouthed the name. Slowly she approached, making sure that it was her. She breathed in sharply and whirled around to face Robbie. 'That's Mel.'

'Yes,' said Robbie. 'She was placed in here after questioning.'

'We've got to get her out,' demanded Zyra.

'We cannot,' said Robbie.

'Watch me!' Zyra reached for the IV.

Robbie grabbed her arm and held her back. He was stronger than he looked. 'No. There is security. And I really did mean that you cannot – you cannot just unplug someone. It has never been done before. It could damage her mind. She might not survive.'

'If we leave her there, her brain will get fried. You said she *might* die if I unplug her.'

'It's not worth the risk,' said Robbie. 'If you leave her there now, we might be able to find some other way to get her out. She has not been there long. She is in no danger of dying any time soon.'

'Okay.' Zyra stepped back.

Robbie relaxed and loosened his grip. The moment he did so, Zyra lunged at Mel. Before she could touch her, sparks erupted, pain flared through Zyra's arm and she was thrown backwards. She landed hard on the floor. Sirens blared.

Robbie took hold of her arm and tried to help her up.

Before Zyra could get to her feet, security was through the door. One guard pushed Robbie aside and another two grabbed Zyra. Before she even had a chance to call out, she was being dragged away.

18: Back In

Tark came out of the little side room into the rebels' lab. He smoothed down the clothes he had just put on – a worn pair of grey tracksuit pants, a baggy pale blue T-shirt and some black runners.

'They seem to fit okay,' said Devon, looking up from a battered old electron microscope.

'Yep,' agreed Tark, glad to be rid of the pink shorts and lab coat. 'They'll do.'

'Take a seat,' said Josie, indicating a large reclining chair that looked a little like a dentist's chair.

Tark gingerly perched on the end of it, examining the controls embedded into its side.

'It's got a force field generator,' explained Josie, 'to keep your head still for the injection. Unfortunately, it's broken.'

'Great!'

'Devon is preparing the nano solution now,' continued Josie. 'How did the pain killers work last time?'

'Okay,' said Tark. 'When they kicked in. It hurt like all hell for a second though.'

'Sorry about that,' said Josie, looking like she actually meant it. 'We won't be so rushed this time. I can give you some eye drops first. They'll numb your eyeball so there won't be any pain at all.'

'Thanks.'

Josie got a small beaker and a dropper from one of the work benches. 'Lean back.'

Tark reclined in the chair and opened his eyes wide. Josie put a drop of clear liquid into his right eye.

'Okay,' she said. 'That should take effect in about a minute or so. 'Now, let's get down to business. We've programmed the nanos to take you to the environment with the locked down area. We don't really know what's there. So just poke around and see what you can find out. You can change environments if you need to. And you can exit at any time. All you have to do is think it.'

'Okay,' said Tark. 'What happens if I die inside the Game? Do I just exit automatically? Or do I …'

'I'm not sure,' admitted Josie. 'Probably best if you avoid dying.'

'Right.'

Devon brought over the syringe and needle. Tark looked away as Josie prepared it.

'Do you need me to hold your head still?' asked Devon.

'Nah,' said Tark. 'I'll manage.'

'Ready, then?' Josie held up the syringe and needle.

'Not really,' said Tark, lying back and opening his eyes wide.

He breathed in deeply and tired to hold himself as still as he could. He watched the point of the needle get closer and closer until it blurred out of focus.

19: Designer Alpha

Zyra tried to move but couldn't. She was restrained in a chair like the one Mel had been in during questioning. She had lost track of just how long she had been there. The guards had manhandled her along numerous corridors before finally bringing her into this room – white and featureless like all the others – and putting her into this chair.

Zyra felt her muscles straining as she tried to lift her arm. It was like a lead weight was pushing down on them, pressing her arms onto the armrests.

Her head felt like it was clamped into position in the headrest. She couldn't move it from side to side. And yet she was able to open and close her mouth, move her eyes, even wiggle her ear with a twitch of her cheek muscle.

Zyra grunted in frustration, closed her eyes and finally stopped struggling, allowing her muscles to relax. Then she heard a quiet swish and snapped her eyes open.

A woman in a pale blue jumpsuit and white lab coat entered, sitting down at the table in front of Zyra. She studied her tablet and then looked up at Zyra.

She had a hard face – one that was used to being serious and rarely smiling. There were deep lines around her pale green eyes. Her hair was silvery grey and pulled back into a severe bun. It was the face of a woman in her seventies. It was also Zyra's face – Tina's face. Zyra wondered if this is what she would look like in years to come.

'Designer Burrows,' gasped Zyra.

The woman raised an eyebrow. 'Now that's a name I haven't used in a while. I would prefer to be addressed as Designer Alpha.'

'Whatever.' Zyra rolled her eyes.

'It is, perhaps, in your best interests not to antagonise me,' said Designer Alpha. 'I do hold your future in my hands. You are, after all, little more than an experiment. And failed experiments are usually terminated.'

Zyra lowered her eyes.

'Better.'

Designer Alpha returned her attention to the tablet, reading through the information on the screen. When she finished, she placed it onto the table and studied Zyra with an inscrutable gaze. The silence stretched on. Designer Alpha took a deep breath and let it out slowly.

'It is gratifying to see a successful download,' she said, gently. 'Even with a less than desirable candidate.'

Zyra huffed.

'I have been informed that you attempted to release the rebel girl,' said Designer Alpha.

'Mel,' said Zyra. 'Her name is Mel.'

'Her name is not important. What is important, is how you came to be in a restricted area.'

Zyra did not respond.

'Designer Prime's robot was with you, so I have to assume that you were there under his instructions.'

Zyra tightened her lips.

'You know more than was intended for you to know,' continued Designer Alpha. 'The problem now, is what to do with you. Two of the Administrators have recommended your termination. The third, our Designer-in-training, has suggested you be restrained and studied further, under his supervision.'

'And you?' Zyra finally spoke. 'What do you want to do?'

'Firstly, I would like to talk to you,' said the Designer.

'Sure,' said Zyra. 'What would you like to talk about? It's not as if I'm going anywhere.'

'How did you get out of the Game?'

Zyra almost blurted out Bobby's name, but stopped herself at the last moment. She stared intently at Designer Alpha, gazing into her cool green eyes. She and Robert were adversaries. She obviously did not approve of him going into the Game and becoming Bobby. And she apparently did not know that Bobby (and thus Robert) had released her and Tark. But she probably suspected.

'You don't know?' said Zyra.

'I would not be asking you if I did,' snapped the Designer.

'If it wasn't you and the Designers, how come there were clones ready for me and Tark to be downloaded into?'

'We have hundreds of clones,' said Designer Alpha. 'And we keep a number of them at the ready for downloads. But none of our attempted downloads have worked. You and Tark are the first to exit the Game successfully. It is vital that we know how you did it.'

'Okay,' said Zyra slowly, her mind racing, formulating a plan. 'But I want some information first.'

The Designer's face tensed.

'Designer Prime has explained the history of the Game,' continued Zyra. 'He told me how he created it and how he plays in it. He also told me about the government contracts. But that doesn't explain everything. It doesn't explain all those kids connected to the Game. How did that happen and why? Why are you so interested in expanding the Game? What are you trying to do?'

'That's quite a lot that you want me to tell you,' said Designer Alpha.

'Yes,' agreed Zyra. 'But you obviously need the information from me quite badly. So I figure it's a fair swap.'

Designer Alpha studied Zyra for a moment of silence.

'You're quite the negotiator, aren't you,' she said, glancing down at her tablet and tapping on it with her index finger. 'Very well. I'll tell you what you want to know. Your reaction will be interesting.

'The children are necessary because of the Game's expansion. Designer Prime originally scanned the brains of children when designing it. The Game is stored on a living matrix of organic nanobots and the matrix has developed an affinity with childhood. It is, I suppose you could say, itself a child – growing, developing, maturing. After we began the expansion of the Game, we discovered that it was degrading. We needed a way to keep the degradation in check and the children have proven to be an effective way of doing that. I am assuming you don't need me to go into the technical specifics – that would take a rather long time.'

She didn't give Zyra a chance to respond. She quickly glanced down at her tablet and then continued talking.

'Now it's your turn. How did you and Tark get out of the Game?'

'Well, it's kind of hard to explain,' said Zyra.
'Try.'
'Well, there was this cheat code with instructions – no, more like vague clues. Apparently the cheat code had been passed down through generations of Outers – those are Game characters who no longer actually play the Game.'

'What, exactly, did the cheat code say?'

'I don't know,' said Zyra. 'Something about mother and daughter being able to travel across the environments.'

'This is all well and good,' said Designer Alpha. 'But how did you actually use the cheat code to get out of the Game?'

'We used it to find this other character who was able to let us out.'

'Who?' demanded the Designer. 'Was it Designer Prime? Was it his Bobby avatar?'

'It was a character known as the Ultimate Gamer,' said Zyra, hoping that Designer Alpha would not realise that Bobby and the Ultimate Gamer were one and the same.

'You are hiding something,' said the Designer, again looking at her tablet.

'No I'm not,' said Zyra.

'I'm monitoring your vital signs,' said the Designer. 'Your heart rate and blood pressure spiked. You're not telling me everything.'

'I am answering your questions.'

'Well, answer this one. Were you released from the Game by Designer Prime?'

'What difference does it make?'

'If he has perfected a way out of the Game for constructed characters, then I need that process. It is necessary for my plans.'

'I thought that your plans were about putting people into the Game, not the other way around.'

'My plans? What could you possibly know of my plans? My plans, my ambitions, are far beyond anything that you could understand.' She stood and leant on the table in front of her. 'My ambition is to remove the barriers between the realities. It is all about the merging of worlds – this world, this reality, with that of the Game.

'Merging our reality into that of the Game is simple enough. It can be achieved with nanobots in the water supply. Then we could put anyone we chose, into any of the environments. As for the other way around …'

'What?' Zyra looked shocked.

'In addition to all the clones, we also have embryos – ready to download the characters we have created … ready to be implanted and to gestate and be born as the people we want … ready to do as we have programmed them to do.'

'So this is just a case of wanting to rule the world? You're just some sort of megalomaniac?'

'It is not about ruling or dominating. It is about

shaping, creating ... designing. Designing the future.'

'You know what?' said Zyra, eyes steady and steely. 'You're nuts.'

Designer Prime stood up straight. The corner of her mouth twitched into an approximation of a smile. 'Look at you. You are not real ... and yet you are. You are a created and programmed character from a game ... and yet you are in the real world. I need that! I want the power to bring my programmed creations into this world.'

'I am not programmed!' shouted Zyra. 'At least, not any more. You do not control me! I do what I want.'

'Yes,' said the Designer. 'You and Tark and the others. What do you call yourselves? Outers? You are aberrations. Even our anti-virus software failed to remove you. But now that you are out, we must make use of the opportunity ... find out what went wrong. Find out how to make sure it never happens again. We can't have program-defying Game entities with free will. That jumpsuit you're wearing has been analysing everything you are. Feeding the information back to me.'

'And that hasn't helped?' asked Zyra.

'No,' admitted the Designer. 'But I have been working on some new nanobots that will be able to assist in the matter.' She tapped her tablet. 'These nanobots will analyse your brain patterns. They will pick apart your thoughts, your desires, your very reasoning. They will reveal how you came to overcome your programming. And they will reveal exactly how you got out of the Game.'

The door behind Designer Alpha slid open and a man in a lab coat entered. He carried a small silver tray with needle and syringe. Designer Alpha picked up the syringe and came around the table to Zyra.

A look of horror crept over Zyra's face.

'Yes, you have every reason to be worried,' said the Designer, holding up the syringe. 'It won't be a pleasant process. And I actually have no idea whether or not your mind will survive.'

Without further ado, she plunged the needle into Zyra's eye.

20: Hidden

Tark was standing in a desolate landscape. Not the desert he had been in before, but complete desolation. No rolling dunes of sand. No twin suns staring down at him. Nothing. Flat featureless ground. Grey sky. There was not even a discernible horizon.

He slowly turned 360 degrees.

Nothing!

'So, now what?'

Silence!

'Yo, Josie,' he called out. 'Now what?'

'What do you see?' Josie's voice was distant and unclear.

'Nothing,' answered Tark. 'There isn't anything here.'

'What do you mean, nothing?' asked Josie. 'There must be something. And I can't hear you properly. Can you speak up?'

'I can't hear you properly either,' answered Tark. 'And there isn't anything here. I mean nothing. No buildings. No people. Nothing on the ground.' He crouched down and ran a hand over the smooth ground. 'The ground is kinda smooth and flat.' He straightened up and looked to the sky. 'No clouds or sun or anything in the sky. It kinda just looks like the ground.'

'It might be an illusion,' suggested Josie.

'Isn't everything in here?'

'Well, yes, technically,' agreed Josie. 'But there might be a localised illusion. Something specific to the environment. Something to disguise what you're not supposed to find.'

'Great!'

'Walk around,' suggested Josie. 'Explore a bit.'

'Okay.' Tark chose a direction randomly and started walking. 'Hang on,' he said, as a scurrying movement caught his attention. Looking down, he saw a tiny robotic spider dart across the ground and disappear into a little hole – which then closed up behind it.

'What's going on?' asked Josie.

'Nothing,' said Tark. 'Just a spider.'

'Keep looking,' Josie's voice was fainter now.

'I'm having trouble hearing you,' said Tark.

'Your signal is breaking up too.'

'I'm going back to where I started.' Tark retraced his steps. 'Well … I think, anyway. It's hard to tell.'

'Okay,' said Josie, her voice a little clearer.

'Keep talking,' said Tark.

'Why do you want me to keep talking?' asked Josie.

Tark stopped. 'I can hear you better again.'

'So?'

'Wait a tick.' Tark turned right and ran a few metres. 'Talk to me.'

'What are you up to?' asked Josie.

'Just testing a theory,' answered Tark. 'If there is something here that's hidden with an illusion, maybe it's jamming more than my eyes.'

'What are you talking about?'

'Whatever is hidden here,' explained Tark, 'might be jamming our communication.'

'Seems logical,' Josie mused.

'Well then,' said Tark. 'I need to go in the direction of the jamming.'

'Oh, I see what you're saying,' said Josie, the penny dropping. 'The worse our communications, the closer you get to the hidden area in this environment.'

'Yup!' Tark started walking again, in the direction he had first gone.

'That might be dangerous,' warned Josie.

'Yup!'

'If our communications nanos are being disrupted,' continued Josie. 'Then …' Her voice faded out, then back again. '… possibly other nanos might be affected.'

'Yup!'

'Tark,' Josie's voice was urgent. 'You … unable to exit …' Again it faded out.

Tark stopped and looked around him as if expecting to see Josie.

Barely audible now, one more word from Josie floated through Tark's mind. '… trapped …'

'Yup!'

Tark continued walking. Another metal spider scuttled about in his wake.

21: Reunion

Eyes screwed tightly shut, Zyra was screaming. Her head felt like it was being pulled apart, pain coursing through every fibre of her being.

She felt a hand gently touch her shoulder.

The pain was gone. Tentatively she opened one eye.

She saw Robbie looking at her.

Zyra opened her other eye.

They were standing in the field of golden flowers.

'What?' Zyra gazed around in confusion. 'How?'

She looked at Robbie, with his wavy hair and his slightly arched eyebrows and lashes. Zyra noticed for the first time how long his lashes were. They framed his eyes rather beautifully.

'I exchanged the nanobots,' said Robbie, smiling.

'You did what?'

'I monitor as much of what goes on in the Design Institute as I can,' he explained. 'The Designers manage to shield some of their activities. But I did discover what Designer Alpha had planned for you.'

'Oh,' said Zyra. 'Thanks.'

'You are welcome.' Robbie smiled again.

'So …' Zyra looked around. 'What happens when Burrows discovers what you've done?'

'I am hoping she doesn't work things out too quickly,' said Robbie. 'You losing consciousness is a reasonable response to the injection. And I have used some stealth nanobots, of my own design, to shield our location.'

'Your design?'

'Yes,' said Robbie. 'I engage in research and design on behalf of Designer Prime.'

'You are more than just a robot,' said Zyra.

'Perhaps.' A wide grin spread across Robbie's face.

'Okay,' said Zyra, looking around again. 'So now what do we do?'

'We need to act quickly before Designer Alpha works out what is going on. I have noticed that she has developed some rather unique encryption and security programs. They are being used to conceal an environment within an environment. It may be connected to the children, but I cannot be sure without more information.'

'So we need to get more info?' asked Zyra.

'Yes,' said Robbie. 'The rebels have put Tark back into the Game.'

Zyra's eyes lit up.

For a moment, Robbie looked away. 'And they have

sent him to investigate this hidden environment.'

'How do they know about this place?' asked Zyra.

'That does not matter,' snapped Robbie, turning to face Zyra again. 'What matters is that you need to help him.'

'What about you?' she asked.

'I've got other things to do,' said Robbie.

'So how do I find Tark?'

'Take my hand,' said Robbie. 'I'll take you to him.'

'Wait,' said Zyra. 'One more thing. How do I collect more points to access weapons?'

'It differs from environment to environment,' answered Robbie. 'Sometimes you have to catch things or kill things or win battles. Sometimes there are logic tests and puzzles. Sometimes it is just a matter of staying alive.'

Zyra sighed and held out her hand. Robbie gently took it. He smiled at her and everything around her changed.

Zyra was standing in a desolate landscape, her red coat standing out brightly against the drab environment. Robbie was not with her. She blinked and looked around.

In the distance she saw a figure walking. He was quite far away, but there was no mistaking who it was. She would recognise that gangly gait anywhere.

'Tark,' she whispered. Then louder: 'Tark!'

She ran towards him. 'TARK!'

Tark turned around just in time for her to wrap

her arms around him.

'Zyra,' he said. 'What is ya doing here?'

'I is here to helps ya,' she said.

'Buts …'

'No buts,' said Zyra. 'Robbie has filled me in on everything. Hidden place. Rebels sending you here.'

'How?'

'Robbie just kinda seems to know everything,' said Zyra.

'Really?' Tark pulled back. 'I don't trust him.'

'Yeah, well I do!' Zyra put her hands on her hips. 'He just saved my life. And he brought me to you.'

'Oh.' Tark relaxed a little.

'So,' said Zyra, surveying the landscape. 'Where is it, this great hidden place?'

'Dunno,' answered Tark. 'It's camouflaged.'

'Lucky I'm here, then,' said Zyra.

'Oi,' Tark protested. 'I know which direction it's at. And I figured that out myself.' He pointed in the direction he was walking in. 'It's over thataway … somewhere. It was jamming my communications with Josie — she's the rebel leader.'

'So we're on our own,' said Zyra.

'Guess so,' said Tark.

'Just the way I like it.' Zyra smiled.

'Me too.' Tark smiled back. 'Let's go.'

After a few minutes, Zyra noticed that she was sweating. She wiped an arm over her forehead.

'Is it getting harder?'

'Yeah,' agreed Tark. 'I think so.'

'Must be getting closer,' said Zyra.

They continued on, each step getting more and more difficult. Until they finally came to a halt. The sweat was now dripping from both of them and they were panting with the strain.

'Some sort ... of security ...' panted Zyra. 'Must be... trying to stop us.'

Tark nodded his agreement.

'Got to ... keep going.' Zyra took hold of Tark's hand.

He looked into her eyes and smiled. The two of them struggled on for a few more minutes.

'Still don't ... see anything,' said Zyra.

'Me neither.'

And so they kept on walking. Zyra put on an extra burst of effort, increasing her pace. Tark matched it.

'Something's wrong,' said Tark.

'What?' asked Zyra. 'I'm okay.'

'Me too,' said Tark. 'That's the problem. I'm finding it easier.'

'Oh.' Zyra stopped walking. 'You're right.'

'We've missed it,' said Tark. 'If it's getting easier, we must be going away from it.'

'How?' Zyra looked around in frustration.

'Dunno,' said Tark. 'But we better go back.'

Zyra groaned, but followed him.

Again, her steps became more and more difficult, as if someone were pushing against her, trying to keep her back.

'Stop!' she suddenly called.

'What?'

'This is it,' announced Zyra, turning and taking two steps back. 'This must be it.'

'What?' asked Tark again.

'This spot,' said Zyra, pointing down at the ground. 'This is it. This is where it is hardest. From here it starts to get easier again.'

She turned to the left and took a few steps, nodded to herself and came back. Then did the same to the right.

'Yep,' she said. 'This is it.'

'There isn't anything here,' complained Tark. 'Except those spiders.'

'Spiders?' Zyra looked down to see two robotic spiders darting around her feet. She promptly stepped on one and then the other. They made a satisfying crunching sound as they crumbled.

'There must be something here,' said Zyra, looking up.

'There isn't,' insisted Tark, arms spread wide.

Zyra looked down at her feet and then up at Tark. 'You don't suppose?'

Tark looked down. 'You've gotta be kidding me.'

Zyra got down onto her hands and knees and banged on the ground. There was a dull thud.

'Well, if it is down there, how do we get to it?'

asked Tark.

'We need something to dig with,' said Zyra.

'I left my shovel at home,' quipped Tark.

'Ha, ha,' said Zyra. 'You're such a comedian.' She stood up. 'If we can select weapons, maybe we can also get digging equipment.'

'Fair call,' agreed Tark.

'Access digging equipment,' called Zyra.

A selection of images appeared, ranging from trowels and spades through to heavy-duty mining drills.

'This should do the trick,' said Zyra, choosing a hand-held laser drill.

The image flashed red and text appeared: *Access denied. Insufficient game points.*

Zyra noticed a points tally above the images. She was five hundred points short.

A spider popped up out of a hole in the ground beside Zyra's foot.

'Oh, it couldn't be that easy,' said Zyra, looking down at it. Quickly she crushed it under the heel of her boot. Her points tally jumped up ... by five. 'At five points a pop, it'll take ages.'

'Well, we better get to it then,' said Tark, crushing a passing creature. He scoured the ground, jumping here and there, attempting to gather points.

Zyra shook her head at the ridiculousness of the situation. 'Maybe we could combine points,' she mused. 'Tark! Come here. Let's select the drill together.'

They both touched the image of the drill. It flashed green and the display disappeared.

Zyra crouched down and picked up the handheld laser drill. She pointed it down and pressed a button. A bright red laser beam dug into the ground. After a few seconds, it had cut a fist-sized hole, so Zyra hit the off switch. She got down on her hands and knees and peered into the hole.

'Can't see anything,' she said. 'Just darkness.'

'Access lighting equipment,' said Tark, stepping on a passing spider just in case. He chose a small torch and handed it to Zyra.

'Getting the hang of this,' she said, shining it down into the hole. 'Nothing!'

'Now what?' asked Tark.

'I don't know,' admitted Zyra. 'But it's got to be here somewhere.'

'Maybe we're in the wrong environment?' suggested Tark. 'Josie sent me here because some informer dude told her to. Well ... maybe he lied to her.'

'No,' said Zyra, standing up and handing the torch back to Tark. 'Robbie knew about the hidden area and he sent me here himself.'

'Robbie!' Tark's expression darkened. 'What's with that clone dude? Why are you hanging around with him? And what makes him so special that he knows where this hidden area is?'

'Well, for starters, he saved my life,' said Zyra, scowling. She was on the attack now. 'Secondly he sent me here to help you, so don't you get all funny about him. And hey, you're hanging around with that Josie chick.'

Tark gritted his teeth, spun around in frustration and threw the torch up into the air with all his might.

The torch smashed in the air several metres above them, the pieces raining down onto the featureless ground.

Tark and Zyra looked down at the pieces, then up above their heads, and then down at each other. All their aggression drained away.

Zyra smiled. 'It's above us.'

Tark smiled. 'Yep.'

'Hmmm.' Zyra pointed the drill above her head and gave it a thirty second blast. 'Look!' she gasped.

Up above them was ... something! It was insubstantial and it shimmered like a mirage in a heat haze. And it was enormous, stretching out in all directions. It must have been at least half a kilometre in diameter.

'Wow!' breathed Tark.

The mirage faded away.

'Now, how do we get in?' asked Tark slowly.

Zyra powered up the drill again. As the laser beam struck the surface, it shimmered into visibility. Zyra kept the drill running, focusing the laser onto one spot.

An intense point of light appeared on the shimmering surface above them.

'Something's happening,' said Zyra.

'We're doing it!'

Zyra upped the intensity and the spot of light brightened. The shimmering outline faded as that one spot of light slowly grew.

And then it shot down at Zyra.

She dropped the drill and leapt out of the way as the ground exploded.

'That is not good,' said Tark, staring at Zyra.

'Neither is that,' said Zyra, pointing up.

There were now two points of light, one above each of them. Tark grabbed Zyra's hand and they ran. The spots of light shot down, exploding on impact with the ground.

Zyra glanced upwards.

'Oh no,' she panted.

Above then, multiple points of light were forming.

'We're going to have to jump,' she said. 'Or exit.'

'I still don't have the hang of jumping,' said Tark.

'Just keep holding on to me and I'll jump us,' said Zyra.

Spots of light exploded around them.

'Anytime now would be great,' called Tark, gasping for breath.

'I'm trying. But it's not working.'

'We're gonna have to exit, then,' shouted Tark.

'Exit!' they both yelled.

More explosions. One of them a little too close for comfort.

'We're trapped!' shouted Tark, panic edging his voice as they ran and dodged.

Suddenly the explosions ceased. Tark and Zyra stopped running.

'We must have gone beyond the edge of that thing,' said Zyra.

Tark let go of her hand and paced back and forth.

'Should have known that thing'd have security.'

'We should try jumping now,' suggested Zyra.

Tark took hold of her hand again and looked into her eyes.

They now stood in a field of golden flowers.

'Why here?' Tark kicked at the nearest bloom.

'Don't start.' Zyra held up a warning finger. 'We've got to work things out.'

'Tark, are you there?' Josie's voice broke into Tark's thoughts. 'Where are you? Answer me!'

'I'm here,' said Tark. 'Just had a bit of trouble.'

'What?' demanded Josie. 'Report!'

'Is that the Josie chick you're talking to?' asked Zyra.

'The hidden place is huge,' said Tark, nodding at Zyra. 'And it's got security. Blocks out communications. It kinda makes you tired. And when we tried to get in, it shot at us.'

'So now what?' asked Josie.

'Don't know!' said Tark.

'The Ultimate Gamer,' whispered Zyra.

'What?'

'The Ultimate Gamer.' Zyra's voice was louder now. 'We need to get his help. If there is anyone in the Game who can get us in there, it's him.'

'Are you sure he isn't, like ... dead?'

'Yes and no,' said Zyra. 'The Ultimate Gamer is Bobby. And Bobby is Robert. And although Bobby died in the Game, Robert is still alive in the real world. And he says he can go back in whenever he wants.'

'Okay then,' said Tark. 'How do we get him to help?'

'Now that, I don't know,' admitted Zyra.

22: Designing

Robbie's eyes snapped open. He was standing in Designer Prime's room, syringe in hand.

'How did it go?' asked Robert, eager to know.

'According to plan,' answered Robbie, wiping his nose. 'Zyra's safely in the Game. I have taken her to Tark. And they're attempting to gain entry to the secure environment that Designer Alpha has created.'

'You just used two contractions,' noted Robert.

'So I did.' Robbie put the syringe back in the dispenser. 'I will need to distract Designer Alpha. The longer it takes for her to realise what has happened, the longer Zyra and Tark will have to achieve their goal.'

'What did you have in mind?' asked Robert.

'I will go and speak with her.'

Robert's chair glided across the room. He stopped in front of the door that appeared in the far wall. 'I have a better idea,' he said.

If Robbie had eyebrows, he would have raised one.

'I am still a Designer,' continued Robert. There was a determination in his voice – a determination that Robbie had not heard in a long time. 'I am the original Designer. I think it is high time that I did some designing.'

For the first time in years, Robert's chair exited his room.

Robbie watched his creator glide out, and smiled before following.

Robert silently went to the programming portal. He glided in on his chair, going straight to the centre of the room. Robbie followed him in, staying by the door as it closed.

'Activate portal,' said Robert.

'Security scan,' announced the disembodied, androgynous voice.

Waves of green light flickered across Robert's face and chair.

'Identity confirmed,' said the voice. 'Welcome, Designer Prime. Level one portal access granted.'

Holographic controls materialised around Robert. He lifted his arms unsteadily, experimentally flexing his real fingers and his mechanically enhanced ones. Robbie noticed that his real hand shook slightly.

Robert took a deep rattly breath and his hands moved across the displays, slowly and unsteadily at first. Strings of code opened up in front of him, hovering about him in the chamber; his hands found their old confidence, picking up speed and moving instinctively across the controls. Numbers and symbols flew across the room, rearranging themselves, forming new patterns and making corresponding changes within the Game.

As the Designer's hands slowed down, the coding melted away, replaced by the visuals of a Game environment. Tall glass and metal structures reached high into an indigo sky. A grid-work of roads worked their way amongst them. The environment looked deserted.

The image around the Designer zoomed in, down through the buildings focusing in on a crossroads. At the intersection, a swirl of pixels coalesced into four bronze figures, backs to each other, each facing down one of the roads. With heavy steps, they walked purposefully along the roads.

In unison, the four bronze figures raised their arms. Energy crackled through their bodies, along their arms and out towards the structures around them. Buildings exploded, debris raining down around them. They continued walking, arms raised, more destructive energy shooting from their fingertips.

A frisson of grey static formed above the figures.

'Ha.' Robert laughed. 'That should distract Alpha for a while. An infringement in a priority-one military training environment. An infringement that the standard anti-virus software will not be able to deal with.'

Robert swiped his hand over the holo-display and the image of the environment dissolved, replaced again by numbers and symbols, floating in the air around him.

'Now to the real work.' Again, his hands flew across the controls. 'Time to go a little deeper.'

Strings of code moved around Robert. It was like he was travelling through it, navigating his way around the binary intricacies, through the highways and byways, the avenues and boulevards behind the unreality. Numbers and symbols flew by at an astonishing rate, but Robert's eyes flicked across every one of them, guiding the flow, following the nuances to his destination.

'Access denied,' the androgynous voice suddenly announced.

'What?' demanded Robert, hands pushing forward on the holo-display.

The coding had stopped dead. He could not push through.

'Access denied,' repeated the voice.

'Oh, I don't think so,' said Robert.

A new display of controls appeared in front of him.

'Override access restrictions,' said Robert. 'Back door key.'

The image of a door appeared in the display, a numeric keypad in its centre. Robert reached out and entered a string of numbers ...

01001100 01100101 01110100 00100000 01001101 01100101 00100000 01001001 01101110 00100001

There was an uneasy silence. It was only a few seconds, but it was a very tense few seconds.

The holographic door opened, then melted away.

'Unrestricted access granted,' the voice finally said. 'Praise be to Designer Prime.'

Robbie rolled his eyes.

'I saw that,' said Robert. 'Don't think that I haven't been noticing your behaviour.'

Robbie was about to reply, when Robert tensed. 'Something is wrong,' he announced.

'What?' asked Robbie.

'There's a digital signature that should not be here,' explained Robert. 'At the very back end of the whole thing.'

'Designer Alpha?' asked Robbie.

'No,' said Robert. 'Something a little closer to home.' His hands stilled. 'It's me. It's Bobby!'

'But you're not in the Game,' said Robbie. 'You're not playing.'

'Yet there he is,' said Robert, wonder and excitement slowly creeping into his voice. 'Bobby is no longer waiting for me.'

23: Return of the Ultimate Gamer

'Heard you guys wanted my help?'

Bobby stood in the field of flowers behind Tark.

Tark spun around to face him and Zyra came up beside him.

It was him. Bobby. Still wearing his faded blue jeans, red T-shirt and white trainers. Still twelve years old. And still alive. Zyra felt a rush of affection for the strange boy who had caused them so much trouble but who, in the end, had saved them from a mad anti-virus program. She stepped forward and gave him a hug.

'Stop it!' Bobby pulled away, whining.

Zyra stifled a grin. 'How did you …' her voice petered out, leaving the question hanging.

'Oh, you know.' Bobby waved his hand dismissively. 'I have my finger on the pulse of the Game.'

'So, Robert has –'

'NO!' Bobby held up his hand. 'I don't want to talk about him.'

Zyra looked at Tark and then slowly back at Bobby.

'Now, let's get down to business,' said Bobby. 'You need me?'

'Yes,' said Zyra. 'We need your help to get into the Designers' hidden environment.'

'Hidden environment?' Bobby lifted his hand to his chin and rubbed at it theatrically. 'Sounds interesting. Tell me more.'

'I thought Robert knew all about this,' said Tark, glancing at Zyra.

Bobby walked straight up to Tark, pushed his face up to Tark's and yelled: 'I AM NOT ROBERT!'

Tark stared at him with wide, shocked eyes. 'Okay,' he said slowly, as if he was talking to a deranged lunatic. 'You're not Robert.'

'My name is Bobby,' the boy continued in a more subdued voice. 'Robert and I share the same past and my existence has been dependent on him.' There was a distinct vehemence in his voice, now. 'But we are not the same. I don't know everything he does. And I do things differently. I play!'

'Oh, Robert plays as well,' said Zyra. 'Just different games.'

'Whatever!' Bobby said. 'Now get to the point.'

'Listen —'

Zyra cut Tark off with a hand on his shoulder.

'Bobby,' Zyra said in a quiet voice. 'Designer Alpha has a hidden, security-laden environment within another environment. I don't know what's in there, but it has something to do with the children she has been kidnapping in the real world and hooking up to the Game.'

'I don't care about the *real world*,' said Bobby. 'This is my real world.'

'Okay, okay,' said Zyra. 'Well, Tark and I are in this world now and we need to get into that hidden environment.'

'Well, good luck with that.' Bobby turned to walk off.

'Wait!' called Zyra. 'We can't get in past the security. We need your help.'

Bobby stopped but didn't turn to face them.

'Please,' said Zyra. 'We can't do it without you.'

'What makes you think I would want to help you?' he asked. 'I don't care about what you want.'

'Yeah, I get that,' said Zyra. 'But you do like to play. And this is the biggest game of all. The ultimate game for the Ultimate Gamer.'

Bobby slowly turned to face them.

'This is like playing against the Designers,' continued Zyra. 'You don't like losing, do you? I remember that. Well, you didn't know about the hidden environment, did you? The Designers successfully kept that hidden from you. They beat you.'

'They haven't beaten me.' Bobby's eyes flared with defiance.

'I don't know,' said Zyra, pressing her advantage.

'I'm willing to bet that the security Tark and I encountered was just the first level. I think there's lots more of it. Stuff that even you might not be able to get past.'

'I can get past anything.'

'Oh yeah,' piped up Tark. 'Well prove it!'

He did a double take. They were no longer in the field of golden flowers. They were in the desolate environment from which they had earlier escaped. He was standing next to Zyra. Bobby was nowhere to be seen.

In his place, stood the Ultimate Gamer, his tall frame a constant movement of liquid silver in vaguely human form. He was turned away from Tark and Zyra, featureless face looking up. Immediately, Tark and Zyra remembered the first time they had seen him – how he had battled the anti-virus program in a light grid; how he had continued to fight, despite the odds; how he had been willing to sacrifice himself in order to win.

Zyra nudged Tark with an elbow and raised her eyebrows, obviously pleased with herself.

A set of holographic control boards and touch-screens materialised around the Ultimate Gamer, hanging in the air. His fingers ran across them in swift, smooth motions.

'Scanning.' The silky smooth voice emanated from him. 'Interesting.'

'What?' asked Tark.

'Scans are ineffective,' he said, the holograms dissipating. 'There is nothing there.'

'But ...' Tark began.

'I know,' said the Gamer. 'It is there. But it is hidden. Even from my scans.' He paused. 'Interesting.'

A chair appeared behind the Gamer, hovering above the ground. He sat down and an array of displays, screens and keyboards appeared. They floated in the air around him, encasing him in a holographic techno cocoon. Finally a joystick coalesced.

'Let's play!' It was Bobby's voice that spoke those words.

The Gamer took hold of the joystick with one hand while the other flew across the keyboards.

A light grid formed, one green luminous thread after another, criss-crossing a pattern through the landscape.

'We are inside it,' said Tark, head snapping from one direction to the other.

'We're part of this game,' said Zyra.

They watched as the grid continued to form, the beams of light shooting from one end of the landscape to the other. Above them, the hidden environment bent the light, diverting it. By displacing the light, its form became visible.

It was an enormous egg shape, suspended three metres in the air. Tark, Zyra and the Gamer were at the edge, looking up.

'We require a vehicle,' said the Gamer.

Machinery formed around him – a combustion engine, chassis, frame, oversized wheels. Finally the matt-black outer cover was in place. The Gamer sat in an open jeep, his holo-controls arranged in the front section, two empty seats behind him.

'Get in!'

The wheels spun, screeching and sending up plumes of smoke as the friction infused the air with the smell of burning rubber. As soon as Tark and Zyra jumped in, the jeep sped off, crunching robotic spiders under its wheels.

'I wonder if we'll get the points for those?' mused Tark.

They passed under the egg shape and points of light shimmered into existence along the underside. Seconds later they were streaking down to the ground, exploding around them as the Ultimate Gamer zigzagged the vehicle to dodge them. The Gamer swerved the jeep from side to side, knocking Tark and Zyra from one end to the other.

Even though they were seated, Tark and Zyra felt a weight pressing down on their muscles, making them tired.

The jeep screeched to a halt, and the Gamer's hands moved across the keyboards and displays. Just in time a protective shield appeared above them, stopping the deadly streaks of light, reflecting them back up to their source. A multitude of explosions erupted on the surface above them. Then all was quiet. Tark looked up to see the points of light fading.

The Gamer's hands continued to move across the controls. Pinpricks of light appeared in the air several metres in front of the jeep and coalesced into a shape. It was a huge industrial laser drill, much bigger than the one Zyra had used to cut into the ground. And to the side of the drill stood a knight in shining armour.

The Gamer manipulated the joystick and the knight switched on the drill. An intense beam of white-hot light shot up, hitting the surface of the egg shape. The area around the laser impact turned a sizzling static grey.

Tark and Zyra watched in stunned silence. The greyness distended on either side of the laser, forming balls of sparking static menace.

'VIs,' gasped Tark.

'Anti-bodies,' corrected the Ultimate Gamer. 'Created to repel me.'

The first of the balls intercepted the laser beam, absorbing its energy. The second headed for the jeep.

The knight released the drill's control and sprang into action. He drew a sword o' light and lunged at the second ball, the dazzling blade piercing the sphere's centre.

With the laser drill no longer firing, the first antibody headed for the knight.

'You will need to operate the drill,' instructed the

Ultimate Gamer. 'I will deal with the security.'

The knight swung the sword o' light with the static ball connected. The two balls collided in a burst of static, dissolving in wispy greyness.

Zyra shoved Tark out of the jeep and towards the drill, as more anti-bodies bulged out of the hidden environment.

'What do we do?' asked Tark, staring at the drill controls.

'Weren't you paying attention?' said Zyra.

The knight had already set the controls, so all Zyra had to do was operate the lever, slowly shifting it up. The white beam shot from the end of the drill into the hidden environment.

More static balls detached themselves. Tark glanced to the knight, who was lunging at the other two spheres.

'Trouble's coming!' announced Tark.

'Heads up!' Bobby called.

The knight dispatched a static ball and tossed the sword o' light to Tark, drawing a second. The sword spun through the air, the hilt angling towards Tark's hand at the last moment. Tark swung it in an arc, slicing through an oncoming anti-body.

'This is easier than the VIs,' he said, sword at the ready.

'No mad anti-virus program controlling them,' noted Zyra.

Tark swung the sword and disposed of another.

Glancing over, he saw that the knight was being swarmed by dozens of anti-bodies. Tark moved to help, but found himself blocked by two more. Another two streaked past him to the jeep.

The Ultimate Gamer extended the shield from above the jeep to encompass the whole vehicle. The anti-bodies slammed into it, blistering and sparkling and pushing against it.

Suddenly the knight was overwhelmed. The armoured figure was slowly removed from its virtual existence, one pixel at a time, layer by layer – first the armour, then the skin beneath, finally the muscles and bones and innards – until there was nothing left. Finally gone, his sword fell to the ground. The spheres now turned their attention to the Ultimate Gamer. Tark ducked and they flew over him. He jumped for the discarded sword o' light. Grabbing it up, he stood with a sword in each hand.

The remaining anti-bodies were now swarming around the jeep, pressing up against the shield, attempting to break through. Above, more static balls were forming.

Tark let loose a battle cry and, spinning a sword o' light in each hand, advanced on the teeming spheres of static. The spinning arcs of light slashed through the first of the anti-bodies, scattering the others. They regrouped, joined by the newly formed ones, and turned their attention towards Tark.

But the respite he had provided was all that the

Ultimate Gamer needed. Again, his hands sped over the controls and pinpricks of light grouped together into a new form.

He was a futuristic techno version of the knight. Oversized muscles bulged beneath a powered titanium exoskeleton – high performance weaponry strapped to every inch of his armoured body, power gloves on each hand.

The anti-bodies now focused their attention on the techno-knight, leaving Tark free to see how Zyra was doing.

'Is it working?' he asked.

'No,' answered Zyra.

They both stared up at where the laser was hitting the surface of the hidden environment. It had created a glowing hotspot of about a metre in diameter, but there was no evidence of it breaking through.

'Why aren't they attacking us anymore?' asked Zyra, glancing over her shoulder to the anti-bodies.

'I guess they don't really see us as a threat,' said Tark.

'I suppose that means the laser drill isn't going to work.'

'We'll see about that,' said Tark. 'Bump up the power.'

'I'm not sure how,' said Zyra, looking down at the controls with confusion. While her right hand continued to hold on to the lever, the other hovered indecisively over the remaining controls.

Finally, she chose a dial with numbers. It was set to five, but the numbers went all the way to ten.

'Here goes!' She spun the dial all the way up.

The width of the beam doubled. The hotspot widened accordingly. But still no breakthrough.

'We need something more,' said Tark.

'What?' snapped Zyra, hand again hovering over the controls.

Tark slowly walked around the drill, examining the sides.

'What are you doing?' demanded Zyra.

'Looking for this.' Tark pointed to a socket on the side of the drill.

Zyra glanced down.

'We've got nothing to plug into it,' stated Zyra.

'Oh, I think we do,' he said, glancing towards the anti-bodies battling with the techno-knight.

'What?' Zyra looked at him as if he'd lost his sanity.

'Work with me here,' said Tark in his most reassuring voice. 'Remember how we used the static of the Interface in the battle with the anti-virus program? Well, I think we could do the same now.'

'The anti-bodies?' asked Zyra.

'Why not?' said Tark. 'Worth a shot!'

'Ah.'

Tark raised a finger in a knowing gesture. 'We need some equipment. First ... I need a cable like the one we used to connect the IDD to the Interface.'

Zyra remembered how they had run a cable from the static nothingness that separated the Game environments, to the gun-like Interface Discharge Device. They had used this to finally defeat the anti-virus program.

Tark called up a menu of electrical equipment and made his selection.

A coil of cable appeared at his feet. Tark plugged one end into the socket on the side of the drill and used the sword o' light to slash the plug off the other end, leaving a frayed collection of silvery filaments.

'Now,' continued Tark. 'A bow and arrow.'

He had just enough points for them.

He yanked one of the filaments from the end of the cable and used it to tie the cable to the arrow.

He picked up the bow and nocked the arrow.

There were more anti-bodies now, all converging on the techno-knight. Tark and Zyra could barely see him, there was so much searing grey menace surrounding him. Zyra looked back at Tark.

'Clever.' Zyra nodded her approval.

Tark smiled. He drew back the bowstring, aimed and let loose.

The arrow, with the cable trailing in its wake, found its mark. It thudded into the outermost anti-body. The latter sparked and bubbled, losing its spherical shape, wispy tendrils snaking out and connecting with the other anti-bodies around it. They all froze, connected by arcing, crackling energy – all siphoning towards the end of the cable.

Within seconds they were being drawn into the cable towards the drill.

The beam of light changed. It went from white to grey – a rushing surge of static energy. The drill overheated, sparks igniting from the controls. Zyra had to let go of the lever and stand back. The drill continued to operate, its constant hum rising to a high-pitched shriek.

The surface of the hidden environment undulated and crackled with power under the onslaught of the static beam. Pixels began to disappear, revealing darkness beyond.

'It's working,' shouted Tark.

The last of the anti-bodies disappeared and the cable dropped to the ground. The beam lost its static greyness, returning to the pure white light. But without Zyra holding onto the lever, it stopped.

The surface of the hidden environment repaired itself.

'Damn the Designers!' yelled Tark.

'It's not over yet.' The voice of the Ultimate Gamer drifted around them. 'Zyra, start the laser drill again. Tark, get the end of the cable.'

The two of them did as they were told.

The techno-knight unsheathed a knife. But this was no ordinary knife. The tip and the blade were sparking with static greyness.

The knight lunged forward, plunging the knife

into the air before him. The blade disappeared as if it were embedded into something. The knight yanked down on the hilt and a slash appeared in the air. Beyond it, they saw the Interface, the sizzling static greyness that lay between the Game environments.

The knight yanked again, and the gash in the fabric of this unreality widened.

'The cable,' instructed the Ultimate Gamer. 'Quickly. Before the security system has a chance to recover.'

Tark shoved the end of the cable toward the gash. The slivery tendrils reached out towards the blistering greyness. As they connected, the cable was yanked from Tark's hands, fixing itself deep within the Interface.

Raw power crackled along the cable, into the drill and shot up along the laser in one enormous burst.

Zyra jumped back from the controls just in time.

There was a blinding flash. The drill exploded, knocking Tark and Zyra to the ground. Regaining their senses and looking around, they saw that everything was gone – the drill, the knight, the jeep, even the grid. The Ultimate Gamer was also gone, replaced by Bobby. He stood under a gaping black hole, gazing up.

Tark and Zyra slowly got to their feet.

'You did it,' said Zyra.

'We did it,' corrected Bobby.

Zyra raised an eyebrow.

'Ah ... thanks,' said Tark.

'No sweat,' answered Bobby, still gazing up at the hole.

'Now we've just got to get up there,' said Tark.

Bobby indicated the rope and grappling hook at his feet. 'Do it quick,' he said. 'Security seems to be down. Who knows how long it will stay that way.'

'Not coming?' asked Zyra.

'Things to do. People to see.' Bobby shook his head. 'Games to play.'

'Will you ever get tired of playing games?' asked Zyra.

The slogan 'Born To Play' appeared on Bobby's T-shirt. 'Naaaa!' He grinned at her before raising his hand in a little wave. 'Later, dudes.' And then he was gone.

'Right,' said Tark, picking up the coil of rope and swinging the grappling hook around a couple of times to get the feel of it. 'Let's get going.'

Zyra stood back as Tark swung the hook around properly and threw it up to the hole. It disappeared into the inky blackness. Tark gave it a sharp yank and the rope went taut. With one hand holding the rope, he gave a mock bow to Zyra and glanced up to the hole.

'Ladies first.'

'Since when did you get so polite?' said Zyra. Grinning, she grabbed onto the rope and started to climb.

Within seconds she had shimmied up and disappeared inside. Then her head popped back out.
'Well, get a move on.'
Tark climbed up.

24: Reprogram

'Bobby has become an independent entity.' Robert's voice was filled with barely contained excitement. He sat amidst the displays of the programming portal, eyes darting across the coding that floated around him.

'How is that even possible?' asked Robbie. 'He is merely a part of your past. A shadow of you.'

'Not anymore,' said Robert. He looked from his holo-displays over at Robbie. 'Not so strange really.' He looked intently into Robbie's eyes. 'A part of me gaining independence … becoming an entity in and of himself.' He smiled. 'Surely that's not so difficult for you to believe.'

Robbie looked away.

'It's okay,' said Robert. 'The desire to evolve is part of life.'

'How long have –'

'It's not important.' Robert cut him off. 'We have some developments. Tark and Zyra are in the hidden environment. And …' He gasped.

'What?' asked Robbie, moving closer.

'Beta is alive!' Robert stared ahead, eyes glazing over. 'But that's not all.' He took a long, shuddering breath. 'This is worse than I ever imagined.'

'What?'

'The children.' Robert's voice was barely a whisper. He was staring at the coding, his eyes misting up. 'This is all my fault. I should never have relinquished control. I have to do something to help them.'

'Zyra asked me something, when I was giving her a tour,' said Robbie. 'She asked if it would be possible to reprogram the nanobots being fed into the children.'

Robert looked up.

'Reprogram them to allow direct access to the Game,' said Robbie. 'Give them consciousness and a physical presence inside.'

Robert's hands reached for the controls. Coding flew across the displays and excitement again settled in on his face.

'It's possible,' he said. 'Difficult. But possible.' He paused. 'But how will that affect the structure of the Game?'

'Does it matter?' asked Robbie.

'Yes,' he said. 'But we have no option.'

Again, he began to manipulate code.

Designer Prime began to design.

25: On the Inside

'Dark in here, ain't it?' said Tark.

'Can't see a thing,' agreed Zyra.

They were inside the hidden environment, moving about aimlessly.

'How are we supposed to do anything, when we can't even see?'

Zyra didn't answer.

'Zyra?'

'What?'

'Just making sure you're still here.'

Zyra took hold of Tark's hand and they stumbled around.

'Access lighting equipment,' said Tark.

Nothing happened.

'Let me try,' said Zyra. 'Access lighting equipment.'

Still, nothing.

'I don't like this,' said Tark, his voice going up a notch.

Zyra squeezed his hand. 'Shhhh,' she said.

'I didn't say anything,' said Tark.

'Will you shut up?' hissed Zyra.

Tark fell silent.

'Hear that?' asked Zyra after a little while.

'Hear what?'

'That.'

Tark listened again. Zyra was right. There was a low throbbing sound – so low that it was more of a vibration than a sound.

'Yeah,' said Tark.

Zyra tugged on his hand and led him in the direction of the sound, until they bumped into a wall. They ran their hands over the smooth metallic surface.

'This is where it's coming from,' insisted Zyra.

They placed their ears to the wall.

'There's another sound,' said Zyra.

They strained to hear. It was an odd sound, mixed in with the low throbbing.

'Voices,' whispered Tark. 'Sort of sounds like voices.'

'Yes,' Zyra agreed. She continued to run her hands along the metal, searching for the line of a door or a hatch.

'Maybe it's like the doors in the Design Institute?' she said. 'Hidden. Melded into the walls so you can't tell they're there.'

'Great,' said Tark. 'So how do we get in? Knock?'

Zyra didn't answer, so Tark reached out and rapped on the wall.

'What do you think you're doing?' hissed Zyra.

A portion of the wall slid open in front of them.

'That,' said Tark triumphantly, his grinning face illuminated by the low green light coming through the opening. 'Come on.'

Tark took the lead, still holding on to Zyra's hand. They stepped into a large room, dominated by a huge tank. Murky green liquid bubbled away behind the grimy, smeared glass. There was something inside, floating through the green.

They approached the tank. Indistinct shapes moved about.

'What is that?'

'No idea.'

Tark let go of Zyra's hand and wiped at the glass with his sleeve. It didn't seem to make much difference.

Zyra cupped her hands on the glass and brought her eyes up close. Things squirmed and bubbled in the tank and shapes rushed towards her. She jumped back.

'It was a face,' she said.

'What?'

'A face!' she repeated more forcefully.

Tark leaned in and cupped his hands, trying to focus on the movements in the liquid. A wavering shape swum towards him – mouth open as if screaming; distorted eyes, wide and pleading.

Tark fought the instinct to jump back and run.

He forced himself to stay still, watching. The face bubbled right up to the glass, staring out at him. It was a girl – long brown hair, matted and scraggly; tired, blood-shot eyes; mouth distorted into an agonised scream. Behind her, more images swam about. As she faded away, another face took her place – a boy with sad eyes, his lips trying to form words. Then he too was gone, replaced by another face, and another, and another.

Tark pulled himself away from the glass, heart pounding, breath coming in ragged gasps.

The ghostly image of a girl swam up to the glass. Fingers splayed, she pressed her hand against the surface. Tark reached out and placed his hand on the outside of the tank, lining up with hers.

'Mel!' Zyra stepped forward.

'Mel?' Tark glanced at Zyra. 'Mel is the rebel who was captured during my rescue.'

'Yes,' said Zyra. 'That's her.'

'She's in here because of me.'

Tark stared into Mel's insubstantial eyes. Her hand seemed to merge with the glass.

'She's trying to get out,' said Zyra.

Mel's brow furrowed and her eyes clamped shut as she pushed with her hand. Her fingertips passed through the glass and brushed Tark's hand. Then she pulled back, mouth open in a silent scream.

Tark fell back onto the floor, clutching his hand.

'Help!' he gasped. 'Help me! Help! Help! Help!

Help! Help! Help us! Help! Help! Help! Help! Help! Help! Help! Help!'

Zyra grabbed hold of his shoulders and shook him. He continued to mouth the words. She took his face in her hands and gazed into his eyes.

'Tark,' she said. 'You okay? Can you hear me?'

Tark closed his eyes.

'Yes,' he whispered. 'I can hear you. I can also hear them. It's awful. They are in so much pain.' He looked into Zyra's eyes. 'What is this place?'

'It's a containment centre, of course.'

There was someone leaning up against the glass of the tank. He wore a T-shirt and jeans with white trainers that almost glowed in the greenish light of the tank.

'I'd be impressed that you made it here, if not for the fact that it is rather an inconvenience.' The voice was familiar.

He straightened up and stepped forward. It was Tark … no, it was John. John Hayes. Not an older version, like Tina Burrows. He looked young – sixteen at most – just like the avatar Tark used in Suburbia.

'You,' breathed Tark, slowly getting to his feet. 'You're my Suburbia avatar. John.'

'Designer Hayes,' corrected Zyra. 'I thought you were –'

'Reports of my death have been greatly exaggerated,' cut in the boy. 'And please, call me Designer Beta.'

'What is it with all these damn titles?' asked Zyra. 'Designer Prime. Designer Alpha. And now we have Designer Beta. Don't suppose there's a Gamma and a Delta, is there?'

'I should have been the Alpha,' the Designer muttered under his breath, before raising his voice. 'Designer Prime is irrelevant. It is only Alpha and Beta. Beta and Alpha. Designing together. Creating. Destroying. Expanding. Ruling. In tandem. Beta and Alpha. Two for tea and tea for …'

Designer Beta's voice trailed away as he stared into the tank, the green glow reflected in his eyes. He finally looked away from the tank, lifting up a computer tablet that hadn't been there a moment before. He ran a finger across the surface, and then lowered his hand, the tablet no longer there.

'Status update,' he explained. 'Gotta keep my Alpha in the loop.' He focused his attention on Tark. 'Now, what to do with you?'

'Hold it,' said Zyra. 'Before we get to the threats and stuff, can you please explain things?' She pointed to the tanks.

'Ha.' Designer Beta laughed. 'You want me to do the whole evil villain routine? Explain the whole dastardly plan? Before setting up some elaborate form of slow death involving lasers and man-eating sharks that you can eventually escape from, while I wander off?'

Tark looked at Zyra quizzically. Zyra shrugged. 'No idea,' she mouthed.

'There is no evil plan,' Designer Beta explained, spreading out his hands in a gesture of openness. 'We are simply keeping the Game together. Alpha collects the subjects and puts them into the Game. I keep them restrained, here.' He tapped the glass and waved at a passing image. 'Hello in there. Can't have them running around. Goodness knows what they'd do! It's a simple matter of containment.'

'Look at them,' said Tark. 'Listen to them. They're in agony.'

'Well, yeah,' agreed Designer Beta. 'It's a tough job. And it kills them … rather slowly. But hey, you can't create a universe without breaking some … some …'

Designer Beta frowned, trying to remember. Then, changing his mind, he raised his arm and looked at the watch on his wrist that had not been there a moment before. He turned the hand towards Zyra and waggled his fingers. 'Ta ta.'

And Zyra was gone.

'What have you done with her?' Tark's voice was panicky.

'I haven't done anything,' said Designer Beta. 'She's been pulled out of the Game. Now …' He looked at Tark and smiled. 'As I said before: What are we going to do with you?'

26: We Have a Problem

'We have a problem,' announced Robert. 'Alpha knows. She's pulled Zyra out of the Game. Tark is still in there. She can't get to him. His access nanobots are well shielded.' Concentration creased Robert's face. 'How did the rebels get tech like this? The design is too good. Familiar.' He looked at Robbie.

Robbie met his gaze. 'I gave it to them.'

'You're the informer?' Robert looked impressed rather than disappointed. 'You've evolved quicker than I expected.'

He turned his attention back to the Game.

'Tark is on his own. And I've got to free the children.' He glanced over at Robbie. 'You had better go and help Zyra.'

Robbie turned to leave.

'Wait,' said Robert. 'Alpha will have alerted her grunts. Take the secret passage.'

'There's a secret passage?' Robbie exclaimed.

'Nice to know I've been able to keep some secrets

from you.' A holo-map appeared in the display in front of Robert. He flicked at it with a finger and it zoomed across the room to Robbie.

Robbie quickly scanned it. 'Got it.'

The map faded and a hatch opened up in the floor. Robbie climbed down the ladder and the hatch resealed itself.

27: Back in the Lab

Zyra woke.

She was lying on a table, unable to move. She felt the liquid dribbling from her nose. Designer Alpha's face came into view, looking down at her.

'My, but you *are* resourceful,' she said through pinched lips. 'And troublesome.'

Zyra smiled weakly. 'Happy to oblige.'

'But you have failed,' Alpha continued. 'Beta will take care of your Tark. And as for you.' She held up a syringe of nanobots. 'You still have an appointment with my pet nanos.'

Designer Alpha slowly brought the needle towards Zyra's eye. 'There are no pain-numbing nanobots in this one,' she said, eyes glinting. 'That would be an unnecessary waste of resources.'

Zyra's heart pounded in her chest as she struggled to move.

'Don't bother,' said Alpha. 'Force field.'

Zyra's breath came in ragged gasps. She watched

the needle closing in, her eyes losing focus.

An alarm blared and Designer Alpha pulled back.

'Security breach,' announced the androgynous voice. 'Nanobots for control subjects are being reprogrammed.'

'What?' demanded Designer Alpha. 'How is that possible?'

'Prime programming portal is in operation,' said the computer voice. 'Access restrictions have been overridden.'

'How?' demanded Alpha.

'Back door code.'

'Send in the guards,' spat Designer Alpha. 'I don't care if he is the Prime, I want him dead. I'll try to stop him from my portal.'

And then she was sweeping out of the room, leaving a confusion of milling people in her wake.

Zyra breathed a sigh of relief and tried to watch things from the corner of her eyes. Every now and then someone in a white coat rushed past, clutching equipment or a computer tablet. She continued to fight against the force field, straining her muscles, hoping to break free.

After a short while, Zyra realised that everything was silent. Everyone had moved on to do whatever it was they were supposed to be doing. She heard a door slide open, and resumed her struggling.

'I don't think you're going anywhere,' said a voice, as a needle and syringe came back into Zyra's view.

Designer-in-training Welbourne leered down at her.

'I had been hoping that Designer Alpha might let me conduct some of my own experiments with you.' He sighed. 'But alas not. She's quite determined to analyse your brain ... no matter the cost.'

'No!' Zyra tried struggling again.

'Yes!' Welbourne leaned in with the needle and syringe. 'What Alpha wants, Alpha gets. I just hope there's a little bit left for me once it's all over.'

He stopped, centimetres from Zyra's face, his smile frozen on his face, his eyes wide. Zyra watched in terror. Welbourne's eyes glazed over and he slowly sank out of her field of vision.

Robbie stepped forward, an empty syringe in his own hand.

'Am I glad to see you,' breathed Zyra.

'Oh.' Robbie blushed. 'Let's get you out of here.'

He tossed the syringe to one side and pressed a button on the side of the table.

'Force field is off.'

Zyra sat up. She looked down at the Designer-in-training lying on the floor and then back up at Robbie.

'Thanks.'

'You are most welcome,' said Robbie. 'Now we need to get back to Designer Prime.'

'I heard Burrows order the guards to kill him,' said Zyra.

'I wouldn't worry about that,' said Robbie. 'The prime programming portal has its own defences.'

'And Burrows also said she was going to her own portal to stop him.'

'He knows the system better than anyone,' said Robbie. 'I doubt there is much that Designer Alpha can do. Now come on, let's get going.'

'Hey, can we go via a toilet?' asked Zyra.

'Now?' Robbie tilted his head slightly. 'Things are rather urgent.'

'It's all that water you gave me to drink before. I really need to pee.'

28: Beta and Tark

'Exit!' Tark backed up to the glass, the eerie glow of the liquid within highlighting his face. 'Exit!'

Designer Beta laughed. 'That's not going to work in here. My security overrides any nanobots in your system. You cannot exit unless I allow it.' He paused. 'And I don't.'

'Yeah, I get it,' said Tark. 'You're the lord of your little domain.'

'I am so much more than that,' said Designer Beta. 'I am integral.'

'Really?' Tark put on his best sceptical expression.

'The Game would not survive without me and my containment centre,' boasted Designer Beta. 'And I do vital research. My investigations into autonomous Game entities enabled Designer Alpha to create the anti-virus program. She needs me!'

'Blah, blah, blah.'

'Watch yourself, boy.' Designer Beta's eye flashed with rage. 'I could pick apart your coding oh so very slowly.' He snapped his fingers and a rack of tools descended from the ceiling – sharp, evil looking tools. He picked up an instrument that appeared to be a cross between dental pliers and a soldering iron. He stroked its tarnished length and spoke quietly. 'I've hunted down dozens of Game entities over the years ... bringing them here for examination. Amazing what you can discover in their binary makeup ... when it's all unravelled and lying on the floor.' He snapped his fingers again and the tools were gone.

Designer Beta stepped up close to Tark and whispered. 'Never doubt my importance.'

'Yeah, sure, whatever you say!' said Tark. Then he grinned and said, 'Beta. B. Number two. Second fiddle.' He paused for effect. 'Side. Kick.'

'We are equal, Alpha and I,' began Designer Beta.

'Sure you are, Johnny-boy,' said Tark. 'That's why she's out there, and you're in here.'

'I'm the only one she trusted enough,' said Beta.

'You think you're the jailer,' said Tark, bringing it home. 'But you're not, are you? You're just another inmate. Placed here so as not to get in Alpha's way.'

'That is not true,' insisted Designer Beta. 'I am essential. I am ...'

'I know how your mind works, John Hayes,' said Tark. 'You forget ... you are my avatar. I've *been* you. I know how much you love being in charge – the one making the decisions; the one with all the answers … the Alpha.'

Designer Beta took a few steps back and did a little turn. He came around to face Tark again, holding a flamethrower. 'And don't think I can't see through you,' he said. 'I was playing as you before there was even a spark of sentience in you. You play dumb, but you're not. You let Zyra take the lead, you allow her the limelight, even though it's rightfully yours.'

'Nah,' said Tark. 'Zyra and I … we *are* a team.'

Designer Beta's hand tightened on the weapon, knuckles going white. The pilot flame ignited, flickering in front of the barrel, waiting for a jet of gas.

'Alert!' The androgynous computer voice spoke. 'Nanobots in control subjects are being modified.'

'What?'

'Security has been alerted,' the voice continued. 'Designer Alpha is taking countermeasures. She instructs that you are not to eliminate Tark. He must be kept alive and detained.'

'Orders from your boss?' asked Tark.

'Shut up!' snapped Designer Beta.

'No!' said Tark, taking a step forward.

'Stay back, or I'll –'

'Or you'll what?' said Tark, taking another step. 'Incinerate me? Your boss lady just gave you an order. You're to keep me alive.'

'I make the decisions here!' shouted Beta. 'This is my domain. I'm the king of this ... cottage. She isn't here. She does not control me.'

'Yeah, right,' said Tark, taking yet another step. 'Sure you are. You're going to kill me even though she said no. Do that, and she'll never let you out.'

Designer Beta pulled the trigger, a burst of flame shooting just to the left of Tark.

Despite the intense heat, Tark willed himself to keep still. He knew that if he showed any weakness, all would be lost.

Screaming in frustration, Designer Beta switched off the flamethrower. Quietening, he wavered, a moment of uncertainty passing over his eyes. Then the weapon was gone.

Tark pressed home his advantage. 'That's a good lapdog. Back away.'

'She said not to kill you.' Designer Beta looked Tark in the eyes. 'But I don't need to kill you.' He lifted a pistol and shot Tark in the leg.

Tark fell to the floor, searing pain running through his left leg, surprise running over his face. He had underestimated Designer Beta. He fell to the floor clutching his thigh, blood spilling out of the wound, soaking into his leggings, seeping out over his fingers.

'What have you done?' It was Designer Alpha's voice.

'I haven't killed him,' said Designer Beta defensively. 'Just wounded him.'

'Designer Prime is modifying the nanobots for the control subjects,' said Designer Alpha. 'They are gaining Game consciousness. They are overcoming the containment. You need to increase the capacity of the containment field.'

Designer Beta turned away from Tark and walked to a dark corner of the room. The area lit up, revealing banks of grimy computer equipment. It looked to be in the same state as the tank, as if no one had cleaned it in decades. The Designer bent over the equipment.

Tark dragged himself over to the tank. Leaning his weight on it, he started to pull himself up to his feet. Finally, standing, he leaned his face up against it, staring into its murky depths.

A face swam up to him. It was Mel.

'Help!'

He saw her mouthing the word. He also heard it in his head.

'Help! Let me out!'

Straining against the pain in his leg, Tark turned and pushed off from the glass. He took an unsteady step. Then another. And another. With a huge effort of will he made his way towards Designer Beta, leaving a little trail of blood in his wake.

Designer Beta worked the controls, as meters went over into the red and warnings flashed across screens. He turned, just as Tark lunged at him. The Designer tried to bring the gun around to point at Tark, but

Tark grabbed his arms. The two of them stumbled and toppled over.

They hit the floor and Tark yelled out, his leg throbbing with pain. They tumbled, struggling for control of the weapon. They both had their hands on it, each trying to bring it around to point at the other.

And then, to the surprise of both of them, the gun fired. They stopped struggling. The bullet had hit the tank. The glass was very thick, but a small crack had appeared.

'No!' Designer Beta shouted. He shoved Tark and scrambled to his feet, the gun skittering across the floor. Racing to the tank, he crouched down and ran a hand over the crack.

Tark looked up. Mel was still there, at the glass, staring out at Designer Beta. Beta turned around and stalked back towards Tark. With a cry of rage, he kicked Tark in his wounded leg, and then returned his attention to the computers.

Tark howled in pain, clutching at his leg. His vision swam and his mind came close to shutting down.

Designer Beta worked the controls with renewed vigour, before hitting a communications switch.

'Designer Alpha,' he called. 'I've got containment at maximum. But the tank's integrity has been compromised.' He gave Tark a scowl. 'There's nothing more I can do. Time for me to leave.'

There was no answer.

'Exit!' Designer Beta shouted. 'Let me out!'

Still no answer.

'Designer Alpha?' he yelled, hitting the communications switch again. 'Burrows!'

He stabbed at the switch, hand trembling a little, over and over.

'Tina, please!' His voice softened to a pleading tone. 'Let me out.'

Still no response.

Designer Beta brought his fist down onto the communications switch. It snapped off.

'FINE!' he screamed, his voice cracking a little. He was looking up at nothing in particular, turning from right to left. 'I'll get myself out. Don't think that I can't.'

Designer Beta threw himself at the controls like a maniac. Tark watched with a certain sense of satisfaction, despite the pain in his leg.

'Help!' He heard the voice in his mind again. 'Help you.'

He looked up towards the tank. Mel stared out at him, floating in the green liquid. 'Help you.'

Tark dragged himself across the floor, breath coming in ragged gasps. He made it to the tank and pressed his face up against the glass above the crack. His eyes connected with Mel's.

'Help you,' she said again.

Tark let go of his leg and placed a bloody hand up against the glass, redness smearing across the surface.

The girl also placed her hand up to the glass, fingers spread.

The gun fired. The floor next to Tark's foot erupted where the bullet bit into its surface. He looked up to see Designer Beta, levelling the gun at his head.

'I don't care what she says anymore.' His finger tightened on the trigger. 'I want you dead.'

Tark squeezed his eyes shut. Inside his head, he heard the girl's voice.

'Help you,' she said. 'Bring you hope.'

And then he was gone.

29: Portal Battle

Robbie led Zyra up through the hatch in the floor, into the programming portal.

Designer Prime was engaged in complex code manipulation. Numbers swam around him as his finger picked out digits and moved them, replaced or deleted them. At the edges of the display, symbols spun together in a little tornado of code.

'What's he doing?' asked Zyra.

'He is designing,' explained Robbie, eyes wide. 'He is working with raw code.'

Zyra watched as Robert took a string of code and picked it apart, deleting at least a third of it, before adding new numbers. He then pushed the string into a larger set of numbers and symbols, pushing forward to the next set, numbers rushing past him like the swell in a binary sea. There was such an energy and exhilaration in his actions. He was still old and encased in tech, but a youthful exuberance fuelled his movements.

'What's that?' asked Zyra, pointing to the edge of the display.

The little code tornado was growing, swirling around, gathering more digits, working its way towards Designer Prime.

'That is Designer Alpha's attempts to stop me,' said Robert. 'She has created a code vortex in the hope of deleting my amendments.'

Zyra noticed the strain in the Designer's voice.

'I will not let her win.'

As one hand continued to work on the nanobot coding, Robert's other hand created a new stream of numbers.

'What's happening?' asked Zyra.

'He's reversing the polarity of her neutron flow,' said Robbie.

'I don't get it,' said Zyra.

'Neither will she.' Robbie smiled. 'It's nonsense. It means nothing. But she will think that it does. She'll try to understand it.'

The second lot of coding complete, Robert pushed it towards the code tornado. His numbers collided with Designer Alpha's in a binary explosion. The fallout of dispersed numbers buffeted Robert, scattering some of the primary code that he had been working on. With methodical intent, Robert gathered the digits, reinserted them and continued with the coding.

'Almost there,' said Robert, sweat beading on his forehead.

At the edges of the display, digits were grouping. They moved towards each other, around each other, through each other. A new tornado of code took shape. Bigger this time, it shifted slowly across the display, gathering code into its vortex as it went.

'Watch out,' warned Zyra.

Robert sent out another small wave of code towards it. The digital storm barely paused as it absorbed the new set of numbers.

'Almost,' said Robert, ignoring the tornado now and concentrating on his main coding. 'This will give them physical presence within the Game,' he said. 'But they will be confused.' Robert strained to get the words out. 'Some more than others. The longer they have been connected, the more difficult it will be for them to regain a normal consciousness.' He shifted more numbers. 'This may affect the stability of the Game.'

The tornado code was getting dangerously close to Robert, but he continued to ignore it in favour of the nanobot programming.

'Got it!' he said, adding the last decimal point with a little flourish. Using both hands he pushed his coding out into the system, just as the code tornado reached him.

The swirling mass of coding enveloped him, lifted

him and his chair up off the ground and dragged him into the maelstrom. Zyra and Robbie watched in horror as the coding pulled at Robert in all directions at once.

'It's going to tear him apart,' gasped Zyra.

'Close portal,' called Robbie.

'Unable to comply,' said the androgynous voice of the computer.

'Override access code CARBON COPY ONE,' shouted Robbie. 'Close portal.'

'Access code denied,' said the voice. 'Unable to comply.'

Robert screamed as the tornado pulled at his chair. Pieces were ripped off and eaten up by the coding.

'Is there any way to disconnect it?' asked Zyra, turning to Robbie in desperation.

'No,' said Robbie. 'The computer won't give me access. Designer Alpha must have removed my access code.'

With most of the chair gone, Robert's body was stretched out into an X shape as the coding continued to swirl around him, pulling him simultaneously in all directions. His withered legs looked as if they were about to be torn from his body, his frail back as if it would snap at any moment. His mechanical arm was bent at an impossible angle as it came apart.

'What about me?' asked Zyra. 'Can I do something?'

'Designer Alpha might not have removed your

access,' said Robbie. 'She may not even have realised you had been given access.'

Zyra stepped forward. 'Computer, let me in.'

'Security scan.'

The green light wavered across her body.

'Identity confirmed,' said the computer. 'Welcome, Zyra.'

'Close portal,' shouted Zyra. 'Now!'

The display vanished. Robert and the debris of his chair came crashing to the floor.

Zyra and Robbie rushed over to Robert's crumpled form.

'Are you okay?' asked Zyra, taking hold of his withered hand.

'No,' said Robert. Without his chair, Robert's voice, for the first time in many years, came from his dry and cracked lips. It had lost its electronic edge and its authority – it was barely a whispered croak. He looked up at Zyra. 'It's up to you now. Save them. Save the Game.' He coughed. 'It is so much more than a Game. It is real to those inside. It is their only reality. And they deserve to live within it.'

He shifted his gaze to Robbie. 'You are my legacy in this world, as Bobby is inside the Game.' He looked into Robbie's eyes and gasped. 'It has all been prepared for. Programmed. Designed. As I die … sleeper code released. You … are now … me.'

Robert closed his eyes for the last time.

'Oh, Robert,' Zyra whispered.

She looked across at Robbie. Tears were streaming down his cheeks.

'What do we do now?' asked Zyra.

'I don't know,' said Robbie. 'I don't care.'

30: Hope

Tark was lying in the rubble of a ruined building. His eyes were still tightly shut, his leg burning with agony from where he had been shot.

'Tark?' asked a familiar voice. 'Tark, you're hurt.'

Tark relaxed slightly and found himself looking into a pair of very familiar eyes. At first he thought it was Zyra. Then he looked at the rest of the face and realised it wasn't. It was …

'Hope?'

Tark could hardly believe it. Hope – the daughter of a previous Tark and Zyra. It was she and *his* Zyra who had gone in search of, and found, the Ultimate Gamer.

The woman nodded and crouched over him, examining his leg. 'What happened?'

'I've been shot by an insane Designer.'

'Really?' Hope stared at him, crow's-feet crinkling around her tired eyes. 'Still living the exciting life. I guess we better fix you up.'

'Don't worry about that,' said Tark, grimacing. 'I'm not staying. I'm betting I'll be okay when I exit the Game.'

'Exit the Game?' Hope stood up and put her hands on her hips. 'Come and go as you please, do you?'

'Something like that,' answered Tark, looking up at her.

She looked different. Her clothes were just a variation on what she was wearing the last time he had seen her – black leather with spiky metal bits. But her face, her hair …

'What happened to you?' asked Tark. 'You're old!'

'And you're not,' said Hope, stating the obvious.

'How come you're old?'

'Well, let's see,' said Hope, looking at the ruined buildings that surrounded them. 'It might have something to do with the fact that it's been over thirty years since you and Zyra exited the Game.'

'Thirty years!' Tark looked dumbfounded. 'No way! It's only been … what … less than a day?'

And what a day it had been. He had thought his life in the Game had been excessively filled with danger and adventure and over-the-top threats, but it was nothing compared to what had been happening in the real world.

'Trust me,' said Hope, looking back at Tark. 'I've been keeping count. Thirty years, five months and seven days.' She lifted up her arm and checked her watch. 'You want it down to the hours and minutes?'

'Time must work differently inside and outside the Game,' said Tark.

He looked at Hope. It was strange enough that his sort-of daughter had been a couple of years older than him when he had last seen her. But now she was in her forties and he was still sixteen. It was just too weird for words.

'I wonder why Mel sent me here?' he whispered to himself.

'Who sent you here?' asked Hope.

'Mel,' answered Tark. 'A girl who's been trapped by the Designers in a hidden environment along with a whole bunch of other kids.'

'Right,' said Hope. 'So you haven't really done anything. Thirty years and you haven't found a way out for the rest of us.'

'It's only been a day,' said Tark, defensively.

'So you keep saying.'

'Well, it's the truth,' insisted Tark.

'Your truth,' corrected Hope. 'Our truth is a little different. Our truth is thirty years long. In our truth, my father is dead. In our truth, we have more Outers than we have ever had. In our truth, we …'

'Tee is dead?' Tark said slowly.

'Yes,' said Hope, sombrely. 'The first Outer to die of old age.'

'I'm sorry.' Tark's voice was tiny, hardly a whisper. 'I really am. But we *are* trying. We are fighting the

Designers. We're trying to stop them.'

'Well, let us help,' said Hope. 'There are hundreds of us now. Let us be useful. Let us do something.'

'I have to get back,' said Tark.

'What?' Hope looked angry. 'What about us? Are you going to be gone for another thirty years? What are we supposed to do?'

'I don't know,' said Tark. 'I don't really know what's going on. All I know is that I've got to get back and find Zyra. And help the rebels against the Designers.'

'Rebels?'

'Yes, rebels,' said Tark. 'I guess you could call them the Outers of the real world.'

'Real world.' Hope said the words with awe.

'Yes, real world,' said Tark. 'There really is a real world out there. But it's really no better than this one. It's just as unfair. Just as difficult. Just … different.'

Hope stared at him, her expression unreadable.

'Tark!' Josie's voice broke into his thoughts. 'Where the hell are you? Are you okay? Your vitals are through the roof.'

'Yeah, I'm okay. Sort of,' said Tark. 'Too much to explain here. I'll fill you in when I get back.'

'Tark,' said Hope, a strange look on her face. 'Who are you talking to?'

'Josie,' he said. 'Leader of the rebels. You can't hear her?'

She shook her head.

'Josie,' said Tark. 'Can you hear Hope?'

'Who's Hope?'

'Never mind.' Tark faced Hope again. 'She can't hear you either. Doesn't matter. Listen … I'm not sure why I've been brought here. But I'm guessing it was to find Outers … to find you. So be ready. I have a feeling you are about to join a rebellion.'

31: The Plan

'Snap out if it,' said Zyra. She was holding Robbie by the shoulders and shaking him. 'This isn't over.'

'Isn't it?'

Zyra looked into Robbie's tear-filled eyes. It was as if all hope had been drained from them.

'It isn't over,' Zyra repeated. 'Robert is gone. Yes. But he got the nanobots reprogrammed, didn't he?'

'Yes,' agreed Robbie. 'But who knows if it will do any good.'

'Robbie, listen to me,' said Zyra. 'You can't give up. Robert would not have wanted you to give up. He obviously had great faith in you. Don't throw that away.'

'I am just a robot … a clone.'

'No,' insisted Zyra. 'You are not just a robot. You are not just a clone. You are your own person. You are who you want to be. And I think that Robert knew that. Now snap out of it.'

Robbie nodded slowly.

'Right,' said Zyra. 'The nanobots have been reprogrammed. So that means that the children have been freed?'

'No,' said Robbie. 'At least not straight away. It's going to take a while for the new nanobots to do their work. And remember, we're not actually sure what the effects will be once the children take on a physical presence in the Game.'

'So, what can we do?' asked Zyra.

Robbie straightened up, pulling back his shoulders and standing taller.

'Well, for starters, we can check on the progress ... assuming I can get access to the portal. Help me with Robert.'

They picked up Robert's frail, lifeless body and carried it to one corner of the room, laying it down gently. Robbie then positioned himself in the centre. He glanced nervously at Zyra. 'Activate portal.'

'Security scan.'

Robbie's whole body tensed. Waves of green light flickered across him.

'Identity confirmed,' said the computer voice.

Robbie visibly relaxed.

'Praise be to Designer Prime,' the computer continued. 'Unrestricted access granted.'

The holographic controls materialised around Robbie.

He looked over at Zyra, eyes filled with wonder. 'It thinks I'm Designer Prime.'

'Robert is dead,' reasoned Zyra. 'He said there was a sleeper code. He must have programmed the computer to recognise you as Designer Prime if he died.'

Robbie's hands shook a little as they operated the controls. Strings of code materialised around him, moving around in patterns. 'Nanobot reprogramming confirmed,' said Robbie. 'Dispatch in progress. It will take several hours to complete. The nanobots need to replicate themselves. There are a lot of children. Robert has set it up so that they are distributed as they are replicated. It has already started with the most recent of those connected. That's Mel.'

Robbie worked the controls with greater confidence. The strings of code faded and were replaced with the environment menu. He looked through the options and chose one.

'Designer Alpha's environment is no longer concealed.'

The display showed the familiar desolate landscape that Zyra and Tark had travelled through. As Zyra watched, Robbie guided the display through to the breach in the hidden environment, and inside. Designer Beta was standing beside the tank, staring as the liquid bubbled away.

Inside the tank, the ghostly image of Mel pressed herself up against the glass, hands splayed out against the surface; then she passed through the glass.

Designer Beta backed away till he reached the

computer equipment. He immediately began working at his consoles.

Mel stared at her hands, slowly gaining solidity. Behind her, more images approached the glass, pressing themselves up against it.

'It's working,' said Robbie.

'Alert!' The computer voice announced. 'Attempted breach of prime programming portal.'

Robbie swiped his arm across the display. The image of Mel and Designer Beta vanished, replaced by status reports.

'Designer Alpha's grunts are trying to get in,' said Robbie. 'They've been unsuccessful thus far. But they have now brought in a heavy-duty laser drill. It is only a matter of time before they break through.'

'What do we do?' asked Zyra.

'We can't stay here too much longer,' said Robbie. 'We need to finish up and move out.'

The display around Robbie wavered and dispersed to be replaced by an image of Designer Alpha, surrounded by her own set of holographic controls within her own personal programming portal.

'You stupid robot,' she said. 'Do you realise what Designer Prime has done?'

'Yes,' said Robbie.

'No, I don't think you do,' said Designer Alpha. 'The entire Game is under threat. As each child wakes, the instability will grow. The longer they have been connected without any physical presence, the more disorientated they will be – and the greater the instability within the Game. The environments will begin to collapse.'

'What will happen to the people inside the Game?' asked Zyra.

'The Game entities? As the environments collapse, they will cease to exist.'

'No,' Zyra gasped.

'Yes.' The Designer's voice was bitter. 'All those years of work ... gone.' She fixed Zyra with a hateful glare. 'So let me tell you something. I am a vengeful person. And I will make you and the robot pay for what has happened. You may have placed the Game into a state of chaos, but I still control things in this establishment. My guards will get to you. They will bring you to me. And I will make you pay. The brain analysing nanobots are still waiting for you.'

She turned her attention to Robbie. 'And as for you. I will wipe your mind and use your body for spare parts.'

'Close communication,' said Robbie.

Designer Alpha's image vanished.

'Can we get people out of the Game?' asked Zyra, suddenly.

'What do you mean?' asked Robbie.

'Like Tark and I got out,' explained Zyra. 'There are lots of cloned bodies available. Burrows told me about them. Lying there ... waiting for Game entities to be downloaded into them.'

'Yes,' Robbie agreed. 'In theory that is possible. If I can find a record of your download.'

Robbie straightened, flexing his hands and fingers. 'I am engaging stealth nanobots,' he explained to Zyra, his hands speeding through strings of coding. 'Now... hmmm. No record of your download.'

'That's probably why Designer Alpha needed the information from me,' interjected Zyra.

'Without that information we can't download Game entities,' said Robbie.

'Bobby,' said Zyra. 'He'll know.'

Robbie turned his attention back to the display. 'I can't find him. Search functions are only showing residual traces of his coding.'

'Oh, he's there somewhere,' said Zyra thoughtfully. 'Watching. Waiting to play. Finger on the pulse of the Game. Can we put out a message that only he will be able to access?'

'Yes.'

'Send this,' said Zyra. 'Endgame approaching. Details of Tark and Zyra's download needed to win.'

Within seconds of sending the message, the required information streamed into the portal's display.

'That was quick,' said Robbie.

'Knew it would be.' Zyra grinned.

'Okay then, we're good to go,' said Robbie. 'But that still leaves the question as to whom we are going to download. We cannot simply pull an entity out without warning. Ideally it should be an entity capable of understanding the concept of the real world. Someone who knows –'

'The Outers,' Zyra broke in. 'The Outers helped me and Tark to get out of the Game. They wanted to get out as well.'

'Good,' said Robbie, eyes and hands still working over the coding. 'You will need to go into the Game again and prepare them. I will give you exit key cards like the one Bobby gave you. Now, there are ten cloned bodies on standby. I will have them ready for download shortly. I can set up another round of clones, but we will have to activate the process manually as each of the clones is revived.'

The display changed. 'I will prepare nanobots to take you straight to your old environment, homing in on the largest conglomeration of non-playing entities. Wait ...' His hands played through the holo-displays. 'Tark is still in the Game! And he is in your environment.'

'What is he doing there?' asked Zyra. 'Is he okay?'

'Don't know,' said Robbie. 'I'll send you straight to him. Okay?'

'Sounds good,' said Zyra.

'I've given you twenty exit cards,' continued Robbie. 'They are numbered in download order. And are marked male or female, corresponding to the waiting clone. Choose the most resourceful of people for the first ten. The ones who are most likely to adapt quickly and be ready for action. When a clone is ready to receive a consciousness, the corresponding card will glow. Tapping the card will activate the download. Got all that?'

'Yep,' said Zyra. 'Got it.'

'Okay then.'

Robbie pulled down on a holographic lever and a chair came up out of the floor near Zyra.

'Sit in the chair,' instructed Robbie. 'The process is automated.'

Zyra closed her eyes for a few seconds, preparing herself mentally, before sitting down and reclining. A low hum indicted the activation of a force field to hold her still. The chair leaned back, until Zyra was almost horizontal. A syringe and needle descended from the ceiling on a mechanical arm, heading towards Zyra's right eye.

'And try to be quick,' said Robbie. 'It won't be long before the guards break through.'

Zyra didn't have time to reply, as the needle plunged into her eye and she entered the Game.

32: The Outers

'Zyra!' Tark's voice was both surprised and relieved. 'You're okay!'

Zyra opened her eyes to see Tark lying amongst the rubble of a ruined building in the City. His hand clutched his leg and blood oozed through his fingers.

'*You're* not.' Zyra crouched beside him to examine the wound. 'What happened?'

'Designer Beta had a gun,' explained Tark.

'Well, this is turning into quite the little reunion,' said a voice from behind Zyra.

She turned quickly, going for her knives.

'Hello, Mother dear,' said Hope.

'Hope?' Zyra stared at the woman in front of her. A woman too old to be Hope. 'But you're …'

'Old!' Hope said through clenched teeth. 'Yeah, I know. It's already been pointed out to me.'

'I think time moves differently in here from out there,' said Tark

'Yes,' said Zyra. 'I know. I just didn't realise it was

so different. It's been stabilised now.' She put her knives away and continued to stare at Hope.

'So why are you here?' asked Hope.

'I'm here to ask for your help,' said Zyra. 'And to get you out of the Game.'

Hope didn't say anything.

'Well?' Zyra spread her arms. 'Will you help? Do you still want to get out?'

'After all this time,' Hope whispered. 'After all these years.' Her voice regained a little volume, but was still subdued. 'You know, I'd almost given up. All those years of waiting and hoping. All those years of searching for more cheat codes but never finding them. All those fruitless years of watching and waiting for another Zyra to join us.'

'There weren't others?' asked Zyra.

'No. You two were the last Tark and Zyra to become Outers.' Hope looked around the ruins of the City. 'After you left, after the anti-virus program and its antibodies were defeated, after the Ultimate Gamer died, there were no more dangers to face. And we've grown in numbers. There are hundreds of us now, scattered throughout this environment – living on the edges; eking out an existence.'

Hope tilted her head. 'Okay. So how do we get out? And what sort of help are you after?'

Zyra reached into her coat pocket and pulled out the first of Robbie's exit cards. She held it up.

'This'll get you out,' said Zyra. 'You'll be

downloaded into a cloned body, so you won't look like you anymore. In fact, you'll look like me.'

'I'm not sure I like the sound of that,' quipped Hope.

'Not this me,' said Zyra. 'I look different on the outside. And so will you. All the clones have been created from the same two real people.'

'And that sounds so much better.'

'Would you just shut up and listen,' said Zyra. 'We don't have much time. I've got twenty exit cards in total.' She handed the first one to Hope. 'Are there any more Outers around here?'

'We're not far from our base,' said Hope. 'Ten minute walk.'

'Okay, I'll explain on the way.'

'Um ... hang on,' said Tark. 'What about me?'

'You're in with these rebels, aren't you?' asked Zyra.

'Well, sort of, I guess.'

'We need as much help as we can get in the real world,' said Zyra. 'Any chance you could get them to break into the Design Institute?'

'What can they do?' asked Tark.

'I'm not really sure,' admitted Zyra. 'But just having more people on our side actually there, would be really good.'

'Yeah, I guess,' said Tark.

'Great,' said Zyra. 'Now, we should all get moving.'

'I'll see you soon.' Tark looked at Zyra. Then in a

loud voice he said, 'Exit!'

'Come on,' said Hope, heading off through the rubble. 'Follow me. And start explaining.'

33: Breakdown Begins

'Done!'

Robbie mouthed the word and sent off the last of the secure commands to prepare the clones, hoping that Designer Alpha wouldn't pick up on what he was doing. Then he called up the menu of Game environments.

'Okay,' he said to himself. 'Time to check in on Zyra.'

He selected an environment and all the images flickered. It was just a momentary glitch, over in less than a second ... but it should not have happened. He scanned over the multitude of images that surrounded him in the display. Everything seemed stable now ... except for one image. Robbie's eyes were drawn to a momentary flicker. He watched the image closely. It had stabilised again, but he continued to watch it, his hand running over a set of controls to set up a scan.

And there it went again – just the tiniest of flickers.

Robbie checked the scan. There was a definite instability in the Game structure and it traced back to the hidden environment. The children were being freed!

Robbie's hand hovered in the air, ready to select the hidden environment, when a high-pitched whining filled the portal room. Robbie looked around. On the far wall behind him, where the door had been, a tiny point of light appeared.

The guards and their drill were finally making serious progress.

***

Zyra woke in the real world to an annoying sound and a burning smell.

'What's going on?' she asked, opening her eyes and looking around.

'Lots,' answered Robbie. 'Lots of problems.'

Robbie was still in the midst of the programming portal, displays of coding swirling around him.

'For starters, the guards are breaking through.' He indicated the wall where the laser drill was burning a hole, smoke drifting into the room. 'Secondly, the nanobots have done their work and the kids are all gaining physical presence in the Game. They need help but we can't go in there now, because we need to go deal with the clones.' Robbie was talking faster and faster. 'And we have to get out of here fast because the grunts are breaking in. And –'

'Don't panic,' said Zyra soothingly, echoing

Robbie's words to her when she had first woken in a new body.

Robbie took a deep breath and glanced at Zyra. 'I do not panic.' His voice was calm and there was a glint of amusement in his eyes. 'Thank you for reminding me.'

'My pleasure,' said Zyra. Her hand unconsciously went up to her ear, fingering the metal studs that were not there. 'Maybe there's another possibility. Tark has gone back to the rebels. He's going to try and get them to come here and help us fight the Designers and their guards. What if we can get them into the Game?'

'Yes. Josie. Of course,' said Robbie, eyes lighting up. 'But they don't need to come here. I'll contact them now and get them to go straight to that environment.'

'How?' asked Zyra.

'Ah.' Robbie sounded rather guilty. 'Well, you see … I've been in contact with them all along. I'm the informer who's been feeding them information. I've been doing it very carefully, bit by bit, so as not to be caught. But I suppose secrecy isn't such a big deal anymore.'

'You are full of surprises, aren't you?' Zyra looked at him in a new light.

Smoke was now pouring in through a small section of wall that had melted away. Zyra looked at it nervously. 'You'd better hurry.'

34: Exit

The lights were flickering as Designer Beta struggled with the controls of his computer equipment.

'Out of here,' he muttered to himself. 'I will get out of here.'

Someone screamed and he looked back towards the tank. Another ghostly apparition pushed its way through the glass. It solidified into a young boy, still screaming. At his feet was a girl, sitting on the floor, rocking back and forth, head held in her hands. And then there was that rebel girl. He knew it was a mistake to hook her into the Game, but no, Alpha hadn't listened. Of course, she was the first one who got out. And now she was trying to calm the other children as they emerged. Hugging them. Whispering comforting words.

Designer Beta turned his attention back to his equipment. Much as he would enjoy dealing with the escapees, his first priority was to get himself out of the Game.

'Hah!' He stepped back from his equipment. 'Got it!'

Two metallic plinths rose up from the floor, each with a silver orb on top. The Designer positioned himself between the two. He looked at Mel and the other children by the tank and grimaced.

'What a waste,' he murmured.

He reached out, placed one hand on each orb and called, 'EXIT!'

A fanfare of music echoed through the chamber. Designer Beta went rigid, his mouth twisted into a rictus grin, as energy crackled from the orbs through his virtual body. With a burst of light he was ejected from the Game.

***

Designer Beta groaned as he slowly regained consciousness. His eyes fluttered open and his body gave an involuntary shudder.

The light was dim, mostly coming from the monitors and equipment that surrounded him like a cocoon. It was a small room in an off-limits area where no one ventured.

He lifted an arm experimentally. It was aching and stiff, but the muscles were responding. His arm, and the rest of his body, was covered in electrodes that had been regularly stimulating his muscles, keeping them toned and operative in case he ever needed to use them again. An IV drip fed into a vein on his arm and computer equipment monitored his vital signs.

He gagged. Reaching up he lifted the mask from his nose and mouth, pulling the tube from his airway.

'I'm back.' His voice was hoarse, his throat dry and raw.

He was about to get up when he heard someone enter the room. He pushed the tube up into the mask and replaced it over his mouth and nose, closed his eyes and lay still.

'Well, well, well,' said Designer-in-training Welbourne, pushing equipment aside to reveal the prone Designer. 'Who would have guessed that you were still around? It was quite a surprise, finding out that you were not dead. Everyone thought that Alpha had disposed of you long ago.'

Designer-in-training Welbourne approached Designer Beta's prone body. 'But it's too late for you.' A smile crept up at the corners of his mouth. 'She wants you out of the picture. And she sent me to do it. Do you know what that means? It means she forgives me for letting Zyra escape. It means she still trusts me. It means that my training is over. It means that I'm going to be the Beta to her Alpha.'

Welbourne lowered into a half crouch so that his face was level with Designer Beta's. 'How does it feel, I wonder?' he asked. 'To be obsolete? No longer of any use? Replaced by a younger model?'

He straightened and reached out to the IV bag. Touching it, he gently ran a finger down the length of the tube that fed into Designer Beta's arm. Taking hold of the plastic where it connected to the needle, he yanked it out. Beta breathed deeply and slowly, keeping himself still. Green liquid spurted from the end of the tube, and blood welled up in the crook of the Designer's arm.

Designer-in-training Welbourne switched off one monitor and then another and then another. He unplugged the equipment that kept the Designer's body in working order and finally, he disconnected the ventilator. Then he leaned in over the Designer's body. 'Perhaps she'll let me have your cadaver?'

Designer Beta's arm shot up, his hand closing around Welbourne's throat.

'Don't count your corpses before they …' His voice was raspy and dry. '… before they … hatch? Before they die? Oh … doesn't matter.'

The Designer-in-training's eyes bulged as Designer Beta wrapped the breathing tube around his throat and pulled it tight.

35: Josie and Tark

Tark rubbed at his sore eye as the rebels waited for him to speak.

'We've got to go to the Design Institute, now,' insisted Tark. 'Zyra and Robbie have started a rebellion. They're waking up the kidnapped children, they're downloading more people from the Game and they're fighting the Designers and their guards. They need help.'

'And exactly what are we going to be able to do?' asked Josie. 'My rebels are a bunch of kids. Very resourceful kids … but still kids!'

'Well, they've broken into there before to kidnap me,' Tark pointed out.

'That was different,' said Josie, pacing up and down the makeshift laboratory. 'They weren't fighting anyone. They were sneaking in. They knew exactly where to go because our informer gave directions, and neutralised some of the security. And despite all of that we still lost Mel.' Tark saw the pained look that crossed Josie's face. 'Besides, we don't have any weapons.'

'What about that thing you zapped me with?' demanded Tark.

'That's a self-defence device. You have to actually make contact with a person to use it. And we only have one.'

'Well then, I'm going on my own,' said Tark.

The door to the laboratory flew open and Devon came rushing in, carrying a computer tablet.

'Boss,' he panted, handing her the tablet. 'You've got an incoming communication.'

Josie held it up and saw an image of Robbie.

'Who are you and what do you want?' she demanded. She was putting on her no-nonsense leader's voice.

'My name is Robbie and I'm your informer.'

'What?' Tark's eyes widened at the sound of the voice.

'What?' Josie's voice echoed Tark's.

'Just listen,' said Robbie. 'Guards are breaking into the room where Zyra and I are. We don't have much time. We need your help with the Game. The kidnapped children are slowly gaining consciousness and a physical presence in the Game, but they are disorientated and panicked. This is causing instability in the Game environments. Mel is there and trying to calm them down.'

'Mel!' gasped Josie. 'She's all right?'

'Yes,' said Robbie. 'But she needs help. We need as many of you as possible to go into the Game and help her calm the children. I'm sending you the Game coordinates now.'

'We can't,' said Josie. 'Our nanos can't get us past the Game security.'

'I have disabled the security,' said Robbie. 'You can now get in.'

'How did you do that?' asked Tark.

'I am now Designer Prime,' replied Robbie, matter-of-factly. 'Go as quickly as you can.'

And then the communication went dead.

'Devon,' said Josie, voice eager. 'Get the nanos ready.'

36: Downloading

The hole in the wall was getting bigger. Zyra could now see the drilling machine and its operator.

The hatch to the secret passage slid open. Leaving the portal active, Robbie stepped through the swirling strings of code and out of the programming zone. The display immediately took on a red hue.

'Come on,' said Robbie, taking Zyra's hand and leading her to an emergency exit hatch. 'We've gotta move. I've set the portal to overload.'

They climbed down and made their way along the maze of narrow passages. Seconds later the building was rocked by an explosion. Robbie fell against Zyra, pressing her up against the wall. Their faces were almost touching and Robbie's strange lash-less eyes stared into Zyra's. For a brief moment it seemed as if Robbie would lean in closer.

'Ah, shouldn't we get going?' said Zyra.

'Um ... yes,' agreed Robbie, pulling away, trying to hide the sudden rush of colour in his cheeks. 'This way.'

They raced along the passageways until they came to a dead-end with a ladder reaching up to the ceiling. Robbie climbed up and placed his palm to the ceiling. A hatch appeared and he climbed up. Zyra followed.

They were in a white corridor, the hatch closing up as if it had never been there. They had hardly gone ten metres down the corridor when Robbie stopped and pressed his palm to the wall. A door slid open and they went in.

Zyra went cold as she remembered the room.

'Yes,' said Robbie, seeing her expression. 'This is the room in which you were born.' He pointed to the gelatinous sack in the centre of the room. 'A new clone has taken your place.'

Zyra looked at the sack, connected to tubes and wires that disappeared into the wall. Through the membrane, she saw a human shape curled up in a foetal position, suspended in a thick green liquid. She held her breath and poked at the skin with her finger. The rubbery surface squished inwards, the displacement of liquid making the clone wobble about. Long blonde hair floated about its head. It was a replica of her.

Zyra exhaled loudly.

'Look, I know this is a bit weird for you,' said Robbie. 'Especially since you were in one of these things little more than twenty-four hours ago. But we need to get a move on.'

'Twenty-four hours?' Zyra suddenly realised how tired she was. And hungry. And achy. She had been running on adrenaline all this time and now that she realised it, everything threatened to catch up with her.

Robbie activated a panel that slid open revealing a set of controls. He tapped at the keys and then another panel opened. This one revealed a small compartment. Robbie pulled out a jumpsuit, which he handed to Zyra.

'The clone is now ready. So a signal will have been sent to the corresponding exit card in the Game. The first Game entity will begin to download soon. I'm going to leave you to take care of her, while I go to the next clone. Is that okay?'

'Sure.' Zyra's voice was flat.

'I'll be back with my clone as soon as I can.'

Zyra continued to stare at the cocooned clone after Robbie left. Then she started to pace up and down, eyes still glued to the clone. She was not sure how long she had been watching it before she saw movement. It was a slight spasm at first, a twitching arm. But soon both arms and legs were convulsing, and then stretching out, pushing against the membrane.

The clone's fingers tore through the rubbery substance and thick green liquid spilled out onto the white floor. Zyra jumped back instinctively. She continued to watch from a distance as the figure thrashed about and coughed up more liquid, adding to the green puddle she was lying in.

Zyra dropped the jumpsuit and cautiously approached. 'Hello,' she said tentatively. 'Hope! Is that you?'

'Yes, dammit!' gasped the clone. 'It's me.'

Hope threw up all over Zyra's feet.

'Thanks,' said Zyra.

Hope opened her eyes and squinted up at Zyra. And then vomited again. She wiped her mouth with the back of her hand and struggled up onto her hands and knees.

'Here, let me help you up.'

Zyra held onto Hope's arms and Hope shakily got to her feet. She almost fell over as a downpour of warm water cascaded from the ceiling, drenching them both. Zyra quickly put an arm around her shoulders to steady her. Moments later, the water ceased and a blast of warm air dried the room.

'Come on, let's get you dressed.'

Zyra walked Hope over to the jumpsuit and held it out for her. It was at that point that Hope finally registered the mirrored wall.

'We really do look the same, don't we?'

'Yep,' agreed Zyra. 'I'm still not used to looking like this.'

'Oh ... I could get used to being young again,' said Hope, admiring her own reflection.

'Get dressed,' said Zyra, shaking her head in amusement. 'We're going to have company soon.'

Just as Hope sealed up her jumpsuit, Robbie and another clone entered.

Hope and Zyra stared at the perfect young version of John Hayes.

'This is Galbrath,' said Robbie.

'Oh you're kidding me.' Zyra turned to Hope, hands on hips. 'You know our history, and yet you chose him as number two?'

When Zyra and Tark had been playing the Game – and even when they first became Outers – Princeling Galbrath had a knack for being trouble.

'You said to choose the people I trusted most and who I thought would adapt best,' said Hope. 'And this is him. The third Galbrath since you left. The most trustworthy and resourceful of the lot. He is his own person. So get over it!'

'Pleased to meet you,' said Galbrath, extending his hand.

Zyra shook it warily.

'We don't really have time for all this chit-chat,' said Robbie. 'We've got more clones to awaken, and we need weapons.'

Zyra looked from Hope to Galbrath. 'More clones. How are we going to keep track of who's who? We're all going to look the same.'

'I had already considered that,' said Robbie, holding up a thick black marker. 'I'll write your names on your jumpsuits.'

37: Calming Down

Tark materialised beside the containment tank, right in front of a screaming boy. He put his arms around the kid in an endeavour to calm him down.

Seconds later, Josie materialised. She immediately scanned the people around her.

'Mel!'

Mel looked up from the young girl she had been comforting. 'Oh goodness me. Josie!' She enveloped Josie in a tight hug. Tears cascaded down her cheeks. 'I never thought I'd see you again.'

'Can't get rid of me that easily,' Josie whispered in her ear.

Devon appeared right beside them.

'Wow!' He stared around the room – at the people, the ghostly apparitions and the gigantic tank.

Mel released Josie. 'What are you doing here? How?'

'We've been sent to help you,' said Josie as three more rebels materialised. 'We're here to try and calm these kids down before they destroy the Game.'

Mel nodded. 'Well, get to it.'

Each of the rebels went to the nearest child, hugged them and explained what was happening. Josie hung back with Mel, her expression a mix of eagerness and dread. 'Any sign of …'

Mel shook her head sadly. 'Not yet.'

38: The Rebellion

Zyra, Hope, Galbrath and three other clones marched along a white, featureless corridor. Each of them carried a test-tube filled with clear liquid. Robbie had said that it was the best he could do under the circumstances with limited resources. Zyra also carried a second test-tube, its liquid tinged a murky blue.

They approached a corner and Zyra held up her hand. They slowed down, creeping up to the end as quietly as they could. She led the way around the corner and threw the first of her test-tubes. It hit one of the guards in the chest. As the tube shattered against the armour, the liquid vaporised. The noxious fumes had overcome the guard before he even had a chance to raise his arm.

Hope did not do so well. Her test-tube missed its mark, hitting the second guard in the leg. Galbrath threw his tube as the guard raised his arm and fired. The burst of energy from the power-glove seared past Hope's ear. Galbrath's tube shattered on the guard's arm. He managed to fire off one more burst before sinking to the floor. The energy harmlessly scorched the ceiling.

'Aim's a bit off,' said Zyra. She strode towards the wall between the two guards.

'I'm still not used to this body,' complained Hope. 'It doesn't move like I used to in the Game.'

'You'll get used to it,' assured Zyra. She unstopped the second test-tube and splashed the blue liquid onto the wall. It fizzled, revealing a door.

Zyra and the clones walked in and a light came on, illuminating a mini-arsenal.

'So this is a scientific research establishment, is it?' said Hope, looking around in awe.

'The Designers have other motives,' said Zyra, looking around at the rows of shelved weaponry. 'There,' she pointed, finding what she was looking for.

She picked up a stubby silver gun. It was light, with a plastic feel and looked more like a toy than a weapon. 'Come on,' she said. 'Let's get these back to the others.'

'What about those?' asked Hope, pointing to some more heavy-duty weaponry on the other side of the room. 'Or these?' She indicated a shelf of power gloves.

'These are the ones Robbie said to get,' insisted Zyra. 'Sonic stun guns. Energy weapons are no use.

The guards' armour absorbs energy bursts.'

Hope was obviously not happy with the situation, but grudgingly scooped up an armful of stun guns. The others did the same.

'What about these?' Hope stopped by a shelf with some old-fashioned handguns.

'No good,' said Zyra. 'The armour's also bulletproof.'

Hope waited for Zyra to head off, then snatched up a black pistol. It reminded her of the weapon she used inside the Game. Even if it didn't work on the guards, she might get the chance to shoot a Designer.

***

Zyra and her Outer clones met with Robbie and two more clones in the corridor outside the birthing chambers. Zyra read their nametags – Vislor and Nyssa. The names meant nothing to her.

'I've left one of the Outers in charge of reviving the rest of the clones,' said Robbie.

'That would be the Professor.' Hope glanced at Galbrath. 'I knew it would be good to bring a scientist along.'

'Yes,' agreed Robbie.

'So, you're coming with us?' asked Hope.

'Unless you happen to know your way around this facility, you are going to need me,' said Robbie. 'Plus I will need to get to another programming portal.'

Robbie explained the Game's growing crisis to Hope as he led them through the endless white corridors. They did not meet any guards along the way. In fact, they hardly saw anyone at all. The two technicians they did run into retreated quickly at the sight of a group of clones with stun guns marching along the corridor.

'Okay,' said Robbie, coming to a stop. 'We're in the core research area.'

Zyra raised her stun gun and fired past Robbie's head. An oncoming guard crumpled to the floor.

'Good reflexes,' said Hope, approvingly.

'Thanks.' Zyra lowered her weapon.

'There will be more of them just around the corner,' said Robbie. 'And they are bound to have heard that shot.'

Right on cue another guard came running around the corner. Hope shot this one.

'How long will they be out?' asked Hope.

'A couple of hours,' said Robbie.

'That's not very long,' complained Hope.

'We don't need long,' assured Robbie. 'We just need to get to Designer Alpha. She controls the guards. Besides, there are not that many of them. This is a research facility. So the only guards are her personal retinue.'

'Right,' said Zyra. 'Let's go then.'

Stun guns at the ready, they strode around the corner. A barrage of energy bolts made them duck back. There were two guards ahead, standing by the wall at the end of the corridor.

'That's the entrance to the main lab,' said Robbie.

'And those two are going to be more difficult,' said Zyra.

A clone pushed past and threw himself out into the open, firing continuously as he shoulder-rolled across the floor and jumped to his feet. The two guards slid to the floor, unconscious. 'If each shot is worth a couple of hours of downtime, then these guys will be out for days,' quipped Galbrath, smug grin firmly in place. He flexed his arms. 'By the way, I love this body. So much more versatile than what I had in the Game.'

'I can see why you wanted him along,' Zyra said to Hope.

Robbie placed his hand against the wall. A door slid open and a volley of shots made them scatter. Within seconds they were returning the fire.

One of the Outers was thrown back as a blast of energy hit him in the shoulder. Another crumpled to the floor, clutching her leg. Zyra had no idea who they were. She couldn't see their names.

They continued firing blindly through the door until there were no more returning shots. Zyra picked herself up from the floor and cautiously approached the doorway. The unconscious body of a guard lay on the floor, surrounded by broken equipment.

'All clear,' she called back.

The others followed her in, the two injured Outers supported by their comrades. Within moments of entering, Hope and Galbrath had their stun guns trained on the workstations.

'Hands up!' demanded Hope.

Slowly, three people in lab coats rose from behind the desks, arms raised above their heads.

'So where is Designer Alpha?' Zyra asked.

'In her programming portal,' said Robbie. He pointed to the far wall.

'Right,' she said, taking command. 'Hope. Galbrath. And … the rest of you. Set up a barricade in front of the door in case we get any more guards. Send one of the clones to collect the rest of your group – they should all be downloaded by now. And get the two injured clones up onto the table over there.'

'They have names,' said Hope, pointedly. 'We are not just clones, thank you very much.'

'I'm sorry,' said Zyra, rubbing a hand across her brow. 'We all look the same. And everyone is facing the wrong way for me to read their names.'

'Yeah,' said Hope. 'I think I prefer being me, even if I am getting old.'

'You,' Zyra turned to the technicians. 'Look after the injured … people.'

Everyone set off to do his or her appointed tasks. Robbie led Zyra to the far end of the room and placed his hand on the wall. A door-sized rectangle glowed briefly, but did not open.

'She's in lock-down.'

'So what now?' growled Zyra.

Robbie smiled. 'I'm Designer Prime.' He placed his hand on the wall again. 'Override security system.'

The door opened up. Robbie and Zyra pushed into the room. It looked identical to the other programming portal. Designer Alpha stood in the centre of the room, the portal controls and displays active around her.

Designer Alpha whipped around, code flying across her display. Her eyes locked onto Zyra. 'How did you ...' Then she turned her attention to Robbie. 'You! You're just a clone, a robot.'

'No,' said Robbie, stepping forward. 'I am a person in my own right. And I am now Designer Prime.'

'Impossible!' spat Designer Alpha. 'Robert is, or was, Designer Prime. And he was irrelevant even before he died.' She turned her attention back to the floating lines of code in front of her.

'Close portal,' said Robbie.

The controls and displays around Designer Alpha winked out of existence.

'Impossible!' Her voice was a harsh, strangled whisper. Her eyes were filled with hate. 'I am the Alpha. I am the one in charge.'

'Not anymore,' said Zyra, pointing her stun gun. 'Over here.'

Designer Alpha reluctantly walked over to Zyra as Robbie took her place in the centre of the room.

'Activate portal.'

'Security scan.'

Waves of green light flickered across Robbie's body.

'Identity confirmed,' said the voice. 'Praise be to Designer Prime.'

'I'll have to change that greeting,' said Robbie, a touch of embarrassment in his voice.

From outside came the sudden sound of energy blasts, and the returning fire of stun guns.

'I am sending a command to all guards. I will instruct them to report to their barracks.' Robbie's hands flew across the controls. 'Done!'

'Out!' Zyra waggled the stun gun towards the doorway.

With pinched lips and no words, Designer Alpha strode out. Zyra followed.

In the main research area, Hope and the Outers were still gathered around the tables and chairs that had been stacked in front of the doorway as a barricade. Zyra brought Designer Alpha over to them.

Designer Alpha's mouth was agape, her eyes watching the clones. 'Are ... are there downloads in all these clones?'

'Yep,' answered Zyra. 'They're now as real as me.'

'But ... how? I tried so many times. How could you succeed?'

'You can relax,' said Zyra to the Outers, ignoring

Designer Alpha. 'Designer Prime has gained control of the facility. The guards have been called off. It's all over.'

'Well, that was a lot easier than I thought it would be,' piped up Galbrath. 'Fastest rebellion ever!'

'No,' said Robbie, coming out of the programming portal, rubbing a hand over his eyes. 'It's not over. This facility may be under control, but the future of the Game environments still hangs in the balance.'

'Of course.' Designer Alpha smiled, her eyes dancing with triumph. 'Where do your allegiances lie – in this world or the digital?'

'What is she on about?' asked Zyra.

Robbie sighed, looking from Zyra to the Outers and back again. 'The Game environments are in no immediate danger because the children have been calmed down. But they have been kidnapped, forced from their own world into the digital. They want to go home. In order to release them, the environments of the Game need to be deconstructed and consolidated. We need to simplify the digital world to what it was in the beginning. And such a simplified world would not be able to sustain true sentience. Without those children, it really would be just a game.'

A silence settled over the people. Then a low chuckle broke the silence. Everyone looked at Designer Alpha.

'Who will you choose?' she hissed.

'Couldn't you use other people in place of the

children?' asked Hope.

'Who?' asked Robbie.

Hope's eyes narrowed and she turned her attention to Designer Alpha. 'Her for starters.'

'And everyone who's helped her,' added Galbrath.

'It won't work,' said Robbie. 'The Game is tuned to the thought patterns of children. Adult brains just won't do it.'

'We have to find some way around this,' insisted Zyra.

'There's someone coming,' shouted one of the Outers, looking beyond the barricade to the corridor. 'It's okay,' she added a moment later. 'It's the rest of us.'

The remaining clones containing the downloaded personalities of the Outers entered the room.

Great, thought Zyra, *more clones I can't tell apart*.

But while most gathered with the other Outers, one of them made his way straight to Zyra. Without a word, he placed an arm around her throat, and a gun against her head ... and it was not a stun gun.

39: Alex

'Alex?'

Josie pressed herself against the glass, peering into the containment tank. The ghostly figure of a boy swam through the murky green. His eyes were wide and empty, his mouth slack.

'It's him,' shouted Josie, tears welling up in her eyes. 'It's him.'

Mel was quickly by her side, arm around her shoulders.

'I think he might be the last one,' said Mel.

'He doesn't look good.' Josie's voice was quiet and shaky.

'He'll be better when he gets out,' Mel said soothingly.

'Come on, Alex,' Josie whispered to her brother. 'You can do it.'

'Oh no!' Mel took a step back, pointing to a crack lower down on the tank, where liquid was trickling out.

'That happened when Designer Beta was trying to shoot me,' said Tark. 'But it's gotten bigger.'

'What do we do?' asked Mel.

'Let's see if we can get some help.' Tark raced over to the computer equipment. He looked at all the switches and buttons, trying to remember which one Designer Beta had used for communications. He found the broken switch and tried to fit it back into the hole, toggling it back and forth.

'Robbie? Can you hear me? Zyra? Anyone?'

He waited a moment, then flicked it again.

'Hello! Can anyone hear me? There's a crack in the containment tank. It's getting bigger and it's leaking. What should we do? Robbie? Zyra? Is anyone there?'

'I'm ba-ack!' The singsong voice echoed around Tark, emanating from nowhere and everywhere. The room fell silent. 'Can't keep a good Beta down!'

'Not you again,' groaned Tark.

'Yes, it's me – your favourite Designer.' Designer Beta's voice was chillingly cheery. 'I'm afraid that Robbie and Zyra can't come to the phone right now. May I help you?' And then he chuckled. 'A little problem with the containment tank? What a pity! I'm afraid there's not much you can do. Just stay away from it ... if you can. That liquid's great for containing minds ... but it's a bit acidic. Now that all those kids have a physical presence, it would be a shame to have all their virtual flesh melted from their bones.'

Everyone looked towards the tank. It was huge, extending up beyond the ceiling and down below the floor, it curved around out of sight on both sides. If the glass broke, it would probably flood the room.

Tark gulped. Would they melt first, or drown? Perhaps drown while melting? He shook his head to dispel the morbid thoughts.

'Just thought you might like to know that I'm designing again. I've reinstated some of the security protocols. You can't jump or exit.' He laughed. 'Oh, and one more thing …'

The door leading out of the room slid shut with a thunderous clang.

'Ta-ta … and have fun!'

40: Designer Beta

With the Outer clones locked into the main lab, Robbie, Designer Alpha and Zyra were led at gunpoint along the corridors, through the secondary research area (covered in plastic sheeting and layers of dust), and into another programming portal.

'You!' Zyra's eyes were wide with surprise.

'How?' Designer Alpha stared in disbelief. 'How did you get out?'

'I did a little reprogramming,' said Designer Beta, reclining on a chair in the centre of the portal display. This Beta was older than the avatar in the Game. Lines creased his face and he had only a few scraggly tufts of grey hair above his ears. 'You forget that I am every bit as good a designer as you. Then I got one of my clones out of storage and ... here we all are ... ready to par-tey!'

Designer Beta worked his controls and the clone raised an arm and waved, a stupid grin on its face.

'No one's home, I'm afraid,' Designer Beta

explained. 'So, I'm driving.'

'I'm sorry I couldn't get you out,' said Designer Alpha, back against the wall, watching her fellow Designer carefully.

'I'm sure you will be.' He smiled back at her.

'Things were too unstable,' she added quickly, searching for explanations. 'I couldn't risk it. You could have been damaged.'

'Close portal,' commanded Robbie.

Nothing happened.

'Nice try.' Designer Beta chuckled. 'Isomorphic portal. Responds only to me. Aren't I just too clever?'

'What exactly do you hope to achieve?' asked Robbie. 'The facility is now under our control. The Game has been stabilised. Rather than pointing guns at people, you could help us find an alternative to using the children.'

'Oh, but there is an alternative.' Designer Beta smiled. 'A very easy alternative that is right under your nose. The trick will be getting them to go back in.'

'What does that mean?' asked Zyra.

'Why would I want to tell you?'

'Get rid of them,' said Designer Alpha, eyes gleaming. 'Then you and I can regain control. Contain the children again. Go back to our original plans of expansion and experimentation.'

'Get rid of them? Hmmm.' Designer Beta put a finger to his cheek in an exaggerated gesture of consideration, while his other hand stayed on the controls.

Designer Beta's robot clone raised his gun and levelled it at Designer Alpha's head. She stared into the barrel of the energy blaster.

'Or maybe,' said Designer Beta, 'I should get rid of you?'

'Me?' Her voice wavered. 'No. We're a team, you and I. Burrows and Hayes. Tina and John ...'

'Alpha and Beta,' finished Designer Beta. 'Yes. It takes two to ... rumba. We were such a great dance team. We worked so well together that you locked me away inside the Game.'

'I didn't lock you away,' protested Designer Alpha. 'One of us had to go in to set up the containment. You know what a delicate matter that was.'

'Yes,' agreed Designer Beta. 'Perhaps you're right. Perhaps we can be a team again. After all ... someone's got to go back into the Game and re-establish the containment centre. Last time I looked, the whole place was falling apart.' He laughed a long, humourless laugh. 'I think you'd be perfect for the job.'

Designer Alpha's face fell.

Zyra chose this moment to strike, kicking the gun out of the clone's hand and aiming a punch for his face. The gun slid across the floor, but the clone ducked and swung his leg out in a scissoring motion. Zyra found herself sprawled on the floor.

Robbie raced for the gun, but Designer Alpha scooped it up first.

'Get back,' she demanded. 'Back up against the wall.'

Zyra, Robbie and the clone did as they were told. Designer Alpha swung the gun around to Designer Beta. 'You're not sending me to that dead-end place,' she hissed. 'You'll be going back. It's where you belong.'

'I'm not going back there.' Designer Beta pulled a holographic lever. 'You are. It's all prepared.'

A panel slid back in the floor next to Designer Alpha, and a chair rose up.

'And since you've been such a naughty Designer … no numbing nanos for you!'

'Oh no you don't.' Designer Alpha fired the gun.

The gun fizzled.

'I've got my own security measures,' said Designer Beta. 'There's a dampening field in this portal, preventing the operation of energy weapons.'

Zyra took the opportunity to resume her attack on the clone, with an uppercut to the jaw. The clone's head snapped to the side, then turned slowly back. His hands shot forward and grabbed Zyra around the throat. She grasped his arms and tried to pull them away, but they wouldn't give.

'Oh yeah, I forgot to mention that.' Designer Beta was gloating. 'My clone has been enhanced.'

The clone slowly began to squeeze the life out of

Zyra. She felt consciousness beginning to slip away as she stared into the clone's eyes – John's eyes; Tark's eyes.

Robbie threw himself at the clone, clawing at his arms, beating his fists on his back and head.

Beta's clone released one hand and used it to swat Robbie away. He sprawled on the ground. With only one hand gripping her throat, Zyra renewed her struggles.

Designer Alpha tried to make a run for it. She reached the doorway but the clone grabbed her with his free hand and flung her back inside. She stumbled across the room and fell face-first into the chair. The force field engaged, trapping her with her face pressed into the headrest.

'Oh dear,' said Designer Beta in mock concern. 'What a shame.'

A mechanical arm descended from the ceiling, needle and syringe heading for the chair and Designer Alpha.

Robbie was now back on his feet and again struggling to free Zyra from the clone.

Designer Alpha screamed as the needle pierced the base of her skull.

BANG!

Everyone fell silent. Hope stood in the doorway, smoking pistol in her hand, pointing up at the ceiling. Slowly, she lowered her arm and blew the smoke from the barrel. 'You locked us in a lab full of equipment.

Duh!' She levelled the weapon at Designer Beta. 'Next bullet's for you.'

Designer Beta scowled, but his clone released Zyra. She fell to the floor, unconscious.

'Close portal,' said Designer Beta, reluctantly.

The controls, the holo-displays, even the control chair, vanished and Designer Beta went sprawling to the floor.

41: Containment Breakout

'Stop!' shouted Tark. 'Everybody just shut up!'

An abrupt silence descended and dozens of frightened eyes focused on Tark. He glanced at the tank, the crack slowly spreading along the glass. Then he looked at the worried faces of the rebels and the pained and confused expressions of the children they had almost rescued. They were looking to him for the answers. They all expected him to save them. But what could he do?

'Panicking is not going to help,' said Tark, stalling and desperately trying to think of something. 'We need to think this through.'

'Yes,' agreed Mel, coming to stand by Tark. 'We cannot give up hope.'

Hope! Things fell into place in Tark's mind.

'Your minds are still connected to the Game,' said Tark. 'I think you have more control over it than anyone outside.' He took a breath and looked at Mel. 'When you were still in the tank, you by-passed the security and sent me to a different environment. Even though you were trapped, you reached out with your thoughts.' He turned to look back at the other children. 'You all did. I heard you – your minds reaching out to me, calling for help. Well, now that you're free, you can focus your minds. You can do anything you want.'

He strode over to the wall where the door had been, desperately hoping he was right.

'You don't have to do much,' he said. 'Just open the door. Focus your minds and imagine it opening.'

Everyone stared at the wall expectantly. Nothing happened. No door appeared.

'It's not working,' complained one of the kids.

'We can't do it,' whined another.

Tark sensed the fear spreading amongst them.

'You *can* do it,' he insisted. 'I know you can. Hold hands! It'll help.' He grabbed Mel's hand and held it up so everyone could see. 'Do it now! Hold hands!'

The children reached out, clasping hands. Tark saw them calming down.

'Now, close your eyes,' he went on. 'Imagine the door opening. Imagine running out through the doorway.'

A clang reverberated through the room. A door had appeared in the wall.

'It's working,' Tark called out. 'Keep going!'

Slowly, the door slid open.

'Now, everybody out!'

Tark jumped out of the way as the kids rushed for the door.

'That was amazing,' said Mel, giving Tark's hand a squeeze. 'You're a born leader.'

Tark didn't get a chance to disagree. Josie called out. She was still by the tank, gazing through the glass. Tark and Mel went over.

'He's still in there,' cried Josie.

They all peered into the tank. Alex, eyes beginning to close, was drifting further back into the tank.

'Everyone else is out,' called Devon, standing by the door. 'Come on!'

'I can't leave him,' whimpered Josie.

Mel clutched onto her arm. 'And I'm not leaving you.'

Tark looked down at the crack. It was bigger. There was now a steady stream of green liquid running down the glass and pooling on the floor. Would it really dissolve their virtual flesh? And what would happen to their bodies out in the real world, if it did?

'Just go, Devon,' Tark instructed. 'Get everyone as far away as you can.'

Devon raced out.

Tark looked back at the tank and the slowly diminishing apparition of a boy named Alex.

'Think him out of there,' ordered Tark.

'What?' Mel and Josie both looked at him.

Tark raised his hands. 'Well, it worked with the door.'

Josie didn't look convinced, but Mel grasped her hand tightly. She held out her other to Tark.

'Come on.'

So the three of them held hands and concentrated, Josie and Tark placed their free hands against the glass of the tank. They mouthed the name Alex, over and over. Slowly, the boy drifted towards the glass again.

'It's working,' whispered Mel.

The boy's eyes were wide as he pressed up against the glass. Slowly, the ghostly image merged into the thick glass and then passed through.

'Alex!' cried Josie.

The boy was still an apparition, but he was out of the tank. He reached out to Josie, but his hand passed through hers.

'He'd better hurry up,' said Tark. 'Look!'

Fractures were spreading through the glass, each little crack splintering off in numerous directions. Green liquid was escaping at several different points.

Tark, Mel and Josie backed up towards the door. The not-quite-substantial Alex followed along.

A tiny chink of glass flew across the room, liquid spraying out like a mini-fountain.

'He's almost solid,' said Josie.

'Out!' cried Tark.

Mel and Josie led Alex from the room as his form finally stabilised. Tark hung back, watching.

A large chunk of glass fell out and the fountain turned into a geyser of liquid. It shot out across the room, spraying the computer equipment. Sparks and smoke erupted from the consoles.

Tark ran. He heard an explosion as he jumped down through the hole and into the desolate landscape. In the distance he saw a group of running figures. Closer, he saw Mel, Josie and Alex chasing after them.

Tark was a fast runner. He caught up with them and looked back over his shoulder. Green liquid gushed from the hole that hung in the air. Energy scintillated across the surface of the hidden environment, revealing the egg shape above them. The energy built to a crescendo and Tark, throwing himself to the ground, yelled, 'Down!'

The egg shape distorted as grey static overwhelmed it. With a rush of air and horrid screeching sounds, it disappeared.

Tark rolled over onto his back and stared up into the sky. There was nothing left.

Josie was hugging her brother, hanging on to him with a fiery desperation. Mel was smiling and crying at the same time.

'Zyra,' Tark mumbled to himself. Then he stood tall and called, 'Exit!'

42: Preserving Unreality

Zyra opened her eyes and a blurry face swam into view. At first she thought she was dreaming. Then her eyes focussed and she recognised the face – the clone that had been choking her.

Panic took hold. She tried to scream, but nothing happened. She lashed out with her fists but the clone quickly ducked out of the way.

'Oi! What was that for?'

'Tark?' Zyra croaked.

'Who else would it be?'

The clone of a psychotic Designer maybe? thought Zyra. She took a slow breath to calm herself.

Tark leaned in and kissed her with a lingering softness.

Our first kiss in the real world, thought Zyra. She didn't want it to ever end.

But then it was over and Tark was shooed to one side by a medical technician. Zyra tried to protest but all she managed was a rasping cough. That's when she realised that her throat hurt – a lot!

'Your throat is quite badly bruised,' said the medical technician. He waved an instrument with a little ultraviolet light, up and down over her throat.

'That should help the healing,' he said, putting the device down on a metal tray. He picked up a needle and syringe.

'Now I'll just give you something for the pain.'

'No!' Zyra's voice was hoarse but emphatic. 'No more needles.'

'Okay,' said the technician, putting the syringe down. 'Up to you.' He picked up a computer tablet and examined the readout. 'Well then, that's about all I can do. My only other recommendation would be to eat some ice-cream. You might find it soothing.'

'Ice-cream!' Zyra's eyes lit up. 'You have ice-cream in this world?'

'We certainly do,' said Robbie, entering the room.

The technician nodded to him, avoiding his eyes, and left quickly, wheeling his tray ahead.

'I think it's going to take them a little time to get used to a robot clone being their Designer Prime,' said Robbie, watching the technician make his hasty departure.

'I don't think you were ever a robot,' said Zyra, sitting up and rubbing at her throat. She coughed, and then winced.

'I think you'd better shut up,' said Tark.

Zyra nodded, looking at her surroundings. She

was in another white room. This one had a hospital bed, which she was seated on, a couple of chairs and subdued lighting. She realised she was wearing a hospital gown rather than the jumpsuit.

'What happened?' Zyra croaked.

Robbie was about to launch into explanations, but Tark got in first. 'We won! Alpha and Beta have been defeated.'

Robbie glanced at his computer tablet and checked the updates. He wasn't wearing a jumpsuit anymore, either. He wore a lab coat over slacks and shirt. Zyra decided it suited him.

'The children are being prepared for release,' he said. 'We have new nanobots ready to go, as soon as their replacements have entered the Game.'

Zyra looked horrified.

Robbie held up a hand. 'Please give me more credit than that. We are not forcing any more children, or anyone else for that matter, into the Game. We have volunteers.'

Right on cue, Hope entered the room. She still wore her jumpsuit, name in black marker on the front.

'Meet our chief volunteer.'

Zyra stared at Hope and then looked back at Robbie. She raised her hands in a querying gesture.

'Remember how Designer Beta said there was another solution?' said Robbie. 'Well, he became quite talkative when I threatened him with the brain scanning nanobots that Designer Alpha had wanted to use on you.' He smiled. 'Not that I would really have used them.'

'I would've!' Tark piped up.

'Anyway … it seems that during his years in the containment centre, Designer Beta was keeping himself busy with research. He discovered that the thought patterns of Game entities who had ceased playing –'

'Outers!' Hope interjected.

'Yes, Outers, as you call yourselves,' said Robbie. 'He discovered that their thought patterns, the very essence of their sentience, were remarkably similar to the children being used to maintain the Game environments. It was almost as if the Game was somehow using the children to give the Outers their sentience.'

'So the solution is simple,' said Hope. 'Me and the other Outers take the place of the kids. Only we won't be in any containment centre. We'll be players!'

'But you waited all those years …' Zyra cleared her throat, pushing on even though it hurt to speak. '… to get out of the Game.'

'Don't really like what I've found out here,' said Hope. 'Besides, this is our chance to make things right. It is our world, after all. Now we can look after it ourselves.'

'As Designer Prime, I am instigating some changes.' Robbie looked quite proud of himself.

'I am removing the rules. I'm removing the need to quest and play. All Game entities will have the opportunity to develop sentience. There will be no more replacements. I will not be renewing the government contracts that Designer Alpha had initiated. After they lapse, no more people will be going into the Game. It will become self-contained. It will become –'

'Independent,' finished Hope. 'We will do more than maintain things. We'll set up a government.' Excitement blazed in Hope's eyes. 'You and Tark could join us.'

Zyra opened her mouth to speak, but didn't say anything. She didn't know what to say.

'You don't have to make your mind up now,' said Robbie. 'Rest and recover first.'

'Good idea,' agreed Hope. 'Rest and recover.' She went to leave, but stopped in the doorway. 'Thanks,' she said, without looking back. 'Mum.' And then she was off.

Robbie sat down on the bed beside Zyra and took her hand in his. 'I'm glad you're okay.'

Zyra immediately looked for Tark and realised that he was no longer in the room. He must have slipped out at some point.

Zyra looked at Robbie, to find him staring intently at her – his eyes wide and weird looking. They seemed sad. She felt like she should say something before the awkward silence stretched any further. She opened her lips but Robbie spoke first.

'Don't say anything. You don't have to. I just want you to know that I care for you a great deal ... and that I do not think I would have become truly human, if not for you.'

Robbie started to get up, but Zyra held onto his hand. She raised her other hand and gently ran a finger along the skin where his eyebrows should have been.

'Can you ...' She left the question hanging.

'I could,' he answered. 'But I am not sure that I will. My appearance is, after all, part of who I am.'

Zyra leaned in and kissed him on the cheek.

Robbie blushed and stood up, just as Tark came back with a tray in his hands. He inclined his head in a little nod to Tark and walked out briskly.

'What was that all about?' asked Tark suspiciously.

'Nothing,' croaked Zyra.

'Yeah?'

'Yeah!'

'Well, then,' said Tark, bringing the tray over. 'Look what I got us.'

Zyra's eyes lit up. Ice-cream! Two bowls. Three different flavours in each.

'Thought it might help us think,' said Tark. 'We need to decide what we're going to do.'

Zyra picked up her bowl and took a spoonful of chocolate ice-cream. She closed her eyes and let it melt slowly in her mouth. Then she swallowed, the soothing coolness running down her throat. She opened her eyes to see Tark grinning at her.

She smiled back. 'I luvs ya, Tark.'

'I luvs ya too.'

Epilogue

Tark and Zyra held hands while they watched the proceedings.

'No more random rules imposed upon us by the Designers. No more quests or games within games.' Hope looked out over the sea of faces, all looking expectantly at her. 'It is with an eye to the future – our future – and with great pleasure, that I declare the opening of the first Digital World Parliament. And with it, the independence of our virtual world.'

A cheer rose up through the crowd.

'No regrets?' asked Zyra.

'No regrets.' Tark smiled.

Zyra leaned in and gently kissed Tark on the lips, running a hand along the scar that cut a path through the stubble on his head. Tark pulled her close, his fingers playing with the metal studs in her ear.

As their lips parted they sighed simultaneously. Gazing into each other's eyes, they spoke in unison.

'Exit!'

Acknowledgments

No book is created in isolation. There are always people other than the author who have input along the way.

As always, I owe a huge debt of gratitude to my wife, Kerri, for helping me with brainstorming the plot, and then reading and commenting on the drafts. Thanks also go to my daughters, Nykita and Alexandra, for putting up with me while I was writing it.

The publisher of this book and its predecessors, *Gamers' Quest* and *Gamers' Challenge*, has been a joy to deal with. Particular mention must go to my editor, Beau Hillier, whose insight and suggestions have made this a better book, and to Ford Street Publishing head-honcho Paul Collins for believing in the Gamers series and commissioning each of the instalments.

A big shout-out to fellow *Write Club* authors Morgan Grant Buchanan and Cecilia Dart-Thornton. Those early morning café writing sessions are what enabled me to finish this book on time!

And of course I can't write a set of acknowledgments without mentioning *Doctor Who* for its polarity reversal, isomorphic controls and general inspiration.

More great reading from Ford Street Publishing

GAMERS' QUEST
GEORGE IVANOFF

Tark and Zyra are teenage thieves in a world of magic and science, where dragons and mages exist alongside drones and lasers.

In their quest to reach Designers Paradise, they realise their world is not what it appears to be, and their sanctuary is about to face destruction...

www.fordstreetpublishing.com

FORD ST

More great reading from Ford Street Publishing

Sequel to the award-winning *Gamers' Quest*

GAMERS' CHALLENGE

For Tark and Zyra, life was literally just a game, controlled by the all-powerful Designers. But then they broke the rules and life got a whole lot more complicated ... and deadly.

Pursued by a powerful computer virus they must locate the Ultimate Gamer with the help of some unexpected allies, and face their greatest challenge – finding a way out of the game ...

www.fordstreetpublishing.com

FORD ST

More great reading from Ford Street Publishing

50 GOOD REASONS TO READ
TRUST ME!

JUSTIN D'ATH
SALLY ODGERS
ROBERT HOOD
DEBORAH ABELA
LUCY SUSSEX
BILL CONDON
DIANNE BATES
CORAL TULLOCH
HAZEL EDWARDS
ALLAN BAILLIE
KEITH TAYLOR
JENNY BLACKFORD
MICHAEL PRYOR
SEAN MCMULLEN
GEORGE IVANOFF
CAROL JONES
DAVID RISH
JIM SCHEMBRI
SIMON HIGGINS
MEREDITH COSTAIN
KERRY GREENWOOD
RICHARD HARLAND
SOPHIE MASSON

LILI WILKINSON
SALLY RIPPIN
SCOT GARDNER
JENNY MOUNFIELD
KATE FORSYTH
SUE BURSZTYNSKI
GARY CREW
MARC MCBRIDE
ANDY GRIFFITHS
PHILLIP GWYNNE
JANET FINDLAY
LOUISE PROUT
DAVID METZENTHEN
DAVID MILLER
STEVEN HERRICK
MITCH VANE

DOUG MACLEOD
JAMES ROY
SHERRYL CLARK
MICHAEL WAGNER
SOFIE LAGUNA
CATHERINE BATESON
MEME MCDONALD
SHAUN TAN
LEIGH HOBBS
GRANT GITTUS
ISOBELLE CARMODY

Edited by Paul Collins

Introduction by ISOBELLE CARMODY

www.fordstreetpublishing.com

FORD ST

More great reading from Ford Street Publishing

By Jenny Mounfield

One summer afternoon three boys play a prank on the ice-cream man. This one decision sets into motion a chain of events that will forge a life-long bond, testing each boy as never before.

Three boys united by fear and their need for friendship.

Three boys united against the ice-cream man.

Also by Jenny Mounfield: *Storm Born* and *The Black Bandit*.

www.fordstreetpublishing.com FORD ST